SHADOW RIDERS

For Matthew:
For all that you will be

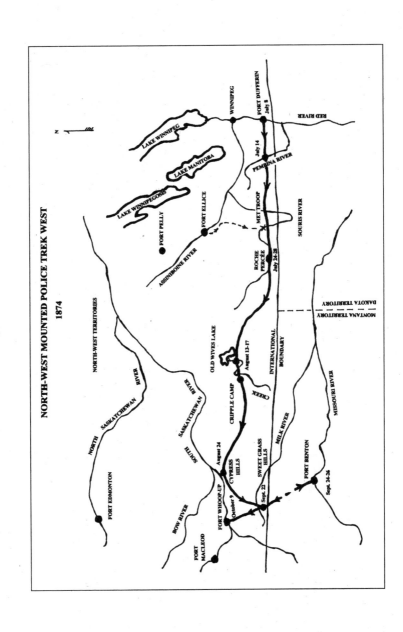

NORTH-WEST MOUNTED POLICE TREK WEST

1874

CHAPTER ONE

The blast of a rifle reverberated through the loft, shattering Rob's dreams. He struggled to sit up and peered around sleepily in the thick darkness. From below, he heard his father's muffled voice, and sounds on the rough floor told him that Luke was sliding to the ladder a few feet away. Fully awake now, Rob reached for the edge of the loft and let his almost six-foot length dangle into the room below before he let go.

He sensed that Luke was beside him as they reached his father, who was peering through the little window at the front of the house. "Get your rifles," he said without turning his head. "Something's been bothering the horses. I'm thinking it's out there still."

Always swift to move, Luke had already snatched his rifle from the hook against the cabin wall by the time

Rob reached for his own. John McCann spoke softly, "Listen to me, lads. I'm slipping over to the barn to take a look. 'Tis more'n likely some varmint in the barn after oats, but Mum thinks she saw somebody hunched over on a horse."

As his father slid through the door, Rob heard him whisper, "If you see something, shoot — but make sure it's not me or one of the horses."

Rob's heart was pounding as he peered through the window at the corral, which was faintly lit by the thin light of the moon. Except for the stamping hoofs and soft snorting sounds from the horses, there was dead quiet. Then the night erupted with his father's furious roar. "I see you, you misbegotten pile of prairie poop! Take the ropes off me horses!"

In reply came the report of a pistol. The corral gate opened, and horses poured through. More shots were fired and, beside him, Rob heard his mother cry out, "John! John!"

Through all of the confusion, wondering if his father was hurt, Rob reacted as he had been taught. Dropping to one knee, he fired blindly into the darkness just above the heads of the fleeing herd. He felt a moment of satisfaction. Above the thunder of the hoofs, he heard a shriek of pain and saw his mother rush over to the barn.

His satisfaction disappeared when his mother's choked voice reached his ears. He raced toward the barn and found her kneeling beside his father who was struggling to sit up, one hand clutching his leg. Luke's bare feet made no sound as he appeared carrying a lighted lantern. Rob gasped at the sight of the blood soaking his father's nightshirt. John spoke through clenched teeth, "'Tis no so bad as it looks."

His comment seemed to spur his wife to action. She rose, dashed into the cabin, and returned moments later with a white scarf. Over her shoulder she said, "I will tie the leg to stop the bleeding. Make a pallet by the fire. The bed is too far for him to be carried."

While Rob gathered blankets from his parents' room, Luke stirred the fire and hung the water kettle from a hook over it and then disappeared. He reappeared from the direction of the barn dragging a wide board. "Good thinking, Luke," Rob said, while his father looked at the board dubiously.

The board wasn't quite long enough to handle John's six-foot-four height, but they managed to slide most of him onto it and carry him inside. When he was stretched on the pallet his wife slit the nightshirt up one side and loosened the knot on the tourniquet. Blood began to seep from the wound again. With a pleased sigh and a smile she turned to the boys. "'Tis but a flesh wound, though he may find it hard to sit down for a time. The bullet went in and out again without hitting a bone." With a glance at Rob she said, "Make tea."

John's face was grey with pain, but he managed a crooked smile. "Honoured I am, to be tied up with your best scarf and drinking tea when 'tis not yet Sunday."

Susan reached down and tugged one lock of her husband's carrot coloured hair.

"'Tis an embarrassment for certain," John muttered, and sighed deeply. "But the least of me worries."

For the first time that night, Luke spoke. "The horses," he said. "Only four are left."

The room grew quiet. Rob knew each had the same thought. Their careful planning and breeding had been for naught, and now they had nothing to sell to buy supplies for the coming winter. He felt a sharp pain in his chest as quick memories of the hours they had spent sweating in the hot sun last year, as they cut the hay and winnowed the oats, flashed in his mind. This was to be their first big lot of horses, which would allow them to buy more than just the bare necessities for the next winter. They had been talking about it for three years.

His thoughts were interrupted when his father spoke to Luke. "Four only," he asked. "Which?"

"The two mares in the barn with their young," was the reply.

"But no Smokey."

Luke shook his head, and John turned his head away without speaking.

Rob sat down slowly. He felt as though a stone the size of a fist was in his stomach. Smokey was the most magnificent stallion this side of Montreal, and the strongest. Susan had taken one look at his silver-grey mane showing brightly against his dark grey coat and named the foal Smokey; and Rob and Luke had helped raise him from the day he was born five years ago. With two mares left they might've had a chance to start again, but without their stallion....

The thought entered his mind as clearly as though someone had spoken. There was but one thing to do: he and Luke would have to find the horses and bring them back.

When he spoke his mother's startled cry of, "Robbie! What on earth are you thinking?" told him it wasn't going to be easy to convince his parents. His father surprised him though.

John struggled to sit up on his pallet, and spoke quietly. "You're but a lad, Rob," he said, "and those were rough men."

Sure of himself now, Rob interrupted. "I'm sixteen, older'n you were when you crossed a whole ocean to work for Hudson's Bay."

His father's mouth crooked in a small smile. "Aye, but I dinna come with a gun in me fist with the intention of tracking down dangerous men."

He raised one hand to forestall Rob's arguing. "I said you were a lad, Rob, but I dinna say you mustn't go. For now, you and Luke are the one bit of hope we have. But you must do this in the manner I am going to tell you."

Rob's tiny mother stood, fists on hips, staring at her husband, her bright blue eyes wide and unbelieving. Avoiding those eyes, John went on: "You and Luke ride down to the fort and tell William McKay what's taken place here. It may be the blackguards will try to sell our horses there, so take care if you see them around the fort."

Rob nodded eagerly. "We'd know the horses all right, and all I'd have to do is give our whistle and Smokey would come running — rope or not."

"Aye, and you'd know the men as well, for I caught a look at one. They wear the same ugly faces that sat at our table and shared our food."

His wife's eyebrows climbed in surprise. "But that was two days ago."

"Aye." Her husband smiled grimly as he spoke. "They must have been hanging about in the woods and planning their thieving."

Rob remembered being uneasy when his father opened the door and bid the five men to enter. It had been raining, and in the warmth of the cabin their damp clothes filled the air with a dank smell. One of the men had lost part of an ear and another — the leader it seemed — had a wide scar from forehead to chin. He had been glad when they finished eating and went on their way.

Luke had been standing beside Rob quietly, and he whirled now and headed for the door. Rob realized he had been hearing a steady sound, which had become the slow beat of hoofs. The two boys shot out of the cabin. Though the sun wasn't yet up, there was enough light now to see six of the missing mares, each dragging a rope as they trotted to the corral. Trailing behind was a saddled horse.

While Luke hastened to close the corral gate behind the tired mares, Rob caught the reins of the other horse. "There's blood on the saddle," he called out.

His mother reached his side and eyed the saddle thoughtfully, "It may be there's someone out there needing help."

When John heard about the blood on the saddle, he smiled grimly. "I say it serves him right." But with his wife's soft cry of "John!" he added. "I'll not have our boys searching for the man. He'll be armed and after

15

being shot, he's sure to be a wee bit touchy. But if perchance they see him along the trail, politely asking for help, they have my permission to bring him here."

Chris, Luke's own horse, was one of those that had returned, but Rob's had not. He was now mounted on one that his mother had named Samantha the day she was born. Rob hadn't said anything for fear of hurting his mother's feelings, but his father had caught his horrified look. "We can call her Sam," he had whispered to Rob. Sam was a bit skittish, but Rob was too comfortable to mind as he rode away in the thief's saddle. It had taken a bit of scrubbing to clean it of old dirt and fresh blood, but it was ten prairie miles better than the lumpy one he had found along the river two years ago. He glanced over at his brother, who usually rode bare back; today he was using their mother's saddle.

Once away from the Assiniboine River flowing along the edge of their land, there was little to hide a man but scrub oak and sagebrush between the cabin and Fort Ellice. By the time they had covered two-thirds of the fifteen-mile trip, Rob began to hope the man had only been winged by the bullet and was riding double with one of his fellow thieves. He wanted to keep the saddle.

Guessing Rob's thoughts, Luke said, "It is the law: what is found on the prairie is yours."

The two boys grinned at each other and urged their mounts into a gentle lope. Both were well aware that — so distant from the Red River settlement — there was no law here. There was little even before the Hudson's Bay Company had been forced to sell their exclusive rights to this land, to the young government of Canada, five years earlier. Even though the Company now owned only a few acres around each of their trading posts, nothing had changed. If you were caught committing a crime and dragged to the nearest Hudson's Bay Company post, the factor there would decide your punishment and carry it out. But crimes often went unpunished, because no one was willing to make the effort to search out the criminals.

With the image of his wounded father and his gentle mother in mind, Rob's jaw set grimly. *This time there will be a search. And it won't end until the men are found.*

CHAPTER TWO

Compared to some of the other Hudson's Bay Company posts, Fort Ellice was small and didn't have a thriving fur trading business. It was important, though, because it was on the Assiniboine River and served as a welcome stopping point on the Carlton Trail for travellers from Fort Garry to Fort Edmonton, all built by the Hudson's Bay Company. Rob's father had worked at Fort Ellice for almost twenty years before the Company agreed to give him use of a few hundred acres of land up the river to raise horses. As part of the agreement, John promised to offer the Company the first opportunity to buy some of his herd, for they were in continual need of horses. This agreement had worked well for the past ten years; John was fair with his prices and his horses were of good stock. If their stolen horses weren't at the fort,

Rob hoped his father's old friends there would be willing to help hunt for the thieves.

Long before they reached the fort, the running horses' trail had been wiped clean by the wind that blew constantly across the hard packed soil. The boys had hoped to pick it up again as they drew closer to the fort. Staring at the ground, they twice circled the tall palisade that enclosed the buildings. They found plenty of hoof prints, but none that indicated a whole herd of horses.

"Lose something, Rob?" a voice called from inside the fort, and the lanky chief factor stepped through the trade room door, wiping sweat from his suntanned face. For a split second, Rob felt like smiling as he recalled the time that — to tease his father — his mother had called McKay an improved Scotsman, because his mother was Cree. McKay was well known for his ability to track man or animal when no one else could, and he had a vast knowledge of the ways of the animals and birds — much of it taught to him by his mother's people. From his father — a partner in the Company — he had received an education and the willingness to work hard.

Rob nodded and slid from his horse. Both boys led their mounts through the gates, and into the sun drenched square lined with low, log buildings. With few words, Rob told the factor about the raid ending with, "We thought they might try to sell them here, but I don't see any signs."

The chief factor tapped his pipe on the bottom of his shoe before responding. "I think we have one of the signs you seek right here — the man you shot. He came riding in without a saddle, hanging onto the mane of his horse. He told a tale about trying to stop an Indian from stealing his horse, and getting shot in the shoulder for his efforts."

Rob's eyes lit up. "Is he still here?"

"He is. Lost too much blood to ride on. Seemed rather annoyed with his companions. They brought him across the river and left him."

Rob and Luke looked at each other. So that's why they didn't find a trail: the horse thieves had driven the herd across the Assiniboine at some point and then crossed the river again to bring the wounded man to the fort.

Rob took a deep breath. "Can we see him?"

"Sure enough," McKay responded. As they walked across the hard packed soil to the far end of the fort, he said, "For a split second, when you rode up, I thought you were your Dad. You're getting so big it seems like you look more like him every day."

Rob grinned. He was pleased to think he looked like his tall, broad-chested father whose flaming red hair had earned him the nickname Big Red from his friends in the fort. Checking to make certain Luke and McKay weren't watching, he squeezed the muscles in his forearm to see if they had grown.

When they reached the small cabin built for the sick, Rob recognized the man instantly. He was the one with the bad ear. Too angry to speak, he listened to the factor question the man. The outlaw denied Rob's accusation, at first. Finally he shrugged and said, "I don't owe them nothing after them going off and leaving me behind. And I don't hold with stealing horses and shooting people."

It was plain that McKay wasn't swallowing the man's efforts to appear innocent. "You were riding with them," he pointed out.

"Not for long," the outlaw blustered. "I just joined up with them down in Benton. We came north for wolf pelts."

Rob and Luke exchanged a long glance. Wolfers! John McCann's thoughts on wolfers were well known after he lost his favourite dog to one of their poisoned buffalo carcasses.

The man denied knowing where the horses were being taken, but he did have one bit of useful information: the leader of the horse thieves was Kamoose Taylor.

When they returned to the factor's office, McKay said, "I heard of this Kamoose Taylor. He's a bad one — giving trouble from Fort Edmonton to the boundary line. I can pass this on to everyone who stops here on the way north. Best you boys stay clear of him."

Seeing their downcast faces, the factor added, "Tell you what, though, lads. I had word of a special bunch of lawmen called the North-West Police," the factor paused and shook his head. "No, it's the North-West Mounted Police. It was made up back east to stop the whiskey traders from selling to the Indians. From what I learned they're in need of horses. My plan is to meet up with them at Roche Percée, with the twelve horses I just bought from the Assiniboines. Might be your horse thieves are of the same mind. For sure I'll know Smokey if I see him. With the North-West Mounted Police there, I wouldn't have any trouble getting the herd back for you. If he's not there, I'll tell your story so they can keep an eye out for the them."

Before Rob could speak, Luke said, "How soon do you go?"

"Not 'til I get word," McKay replied. "One of my men — Patrick Moss — left Dufferin with the troops. He said it took them all day to go eight miles. At that rate it may be some time before they get to Roche Percée, but to make certain I sent him back to get another report on their progress."

A glance at Luke told Rob his adopted brother was as disappointed as he was with this information. While he wondered what to do next, Luke asked, "How many police?"

The factor replied, "About three hundred — half waited at Fort Dufferin for the other half that came by train from far and away back east, along with all the supplies and special horses for the journey."

That information piqued Rob's curiosity. "What kind of special horses?"

McKay smiled ruefully, "I think he meant special in the wrong way for the journey they're undertaking. Patrick said that the column is a grand sight with the men in red jackets and little red hats and white gloves, and each troop on its own colour horse. The column stretches out more than a mile, with about two hundred carts and wagons bringing up the rear. The trouble is they have field guns — each weigh a ton — and the horses have a lot of trouble pulling them unless the trail's smooth and flat."

"Wonder who dreamed that up," Rob said.

"He doesn't know for certain, but Patrick believes it was the man in charge — Colonel French. He seemed to be peacock proud of the look of his men and their horses."

"We could have sold about twenty to them, had they not been stolen," Rob said trying not to show the despair he felt.

"How long does it take to ride to Roche Percée?" Luke asked.

McKay reached for a rough map lying on his desk. He pointed to the X marking Fort Ellice, and then pressed down the broad tip of his thumb to roughly measure the trail to Roche Percée. "It's about a hundred miles, so two or three days in good weather."

Both boys stared at the map as Luke traced the line of the Assiniboine River where it dipped south. Then they raised their heads to look at each other.

Darting a glance from one to the other, the factor snapped, "Don't even think about it! You'll get no boat here to take down the river!"

"We have horses, Mr. McKay, and don't need a boat," Rob said. "But we'd be much obliged if you could let us have some supplies to be paid for later."

The factor frowned. "You must be daft, lad. You would be riding near a hundred miles and more than likely find that you missed the red-coated men."

With growing excitement at the prospect of doing something that might lead to the recovery of Smokey and the herd, Rob grinned in approval as Luke said, "That is true, Mr. McKay, but that many men and horses and wagons would leave a wide trail — easy to follow even if it rains buckets."

McKay shook his head, seeing it was useless to argue. "Well then, I won't refuse to give you supplies and a note for Patrick Moss, who will help you if he can. Other than that, I will send word to your father. I won't go myself because I don't want to be the one to break this bit of news to him."

They had been riding for almost four hours when Rob turned Sam down a deer trail leading through the thick scrub lining the river. Wordlessly, Luke followed. While they slipped off their boots to step into the edge of the stream and fill their canteens, Sam, Chris, and the pack horse eagerly lapped the bitingly cold water. His canteen full, Rob backed up to a flat rock and looked over at the high-cheek-boned face of his dark-haired, dark-skinned brother. It was then that he was hit by the enormity of what they were attempting.

Luke's only about thirteen, and not near as big as me, and skinny besides — strong, though, almost as strong as me. Long as I can remember he'd try to do everything that I could. I didn't even have to ask him to come, because we always do everything together. Just the same: win or lose, Dad's going to have my hide when we get home.

Luke moved closer and squatted on his heels. Squinting into the sun, he said, "We best get moving — only about two hours to sundown."

Rob nodded and stretched, determined not to let Luke sense his misgivings. Gesturing at the three horses, he said, "You'll do just fine with Chris to ride. Don't know what I was thinking when I saddled up Sam. She's still mighty flighty. Another thing: we could have made better time without the pack horse."

Luke's quick grin was followed by a jab at Rob's ribs. "And without the pack horse, tonight you'd have the sky for a blanket and a saddle for a pillow, and I would have to listen all night to your complaining."

Rob's response was to slap Luke's bottom with his hat, "Just for that, you can be the one to lead it."

As they made camp that night, Rob admitted to himself that, impatient as he had been to leave the fort, he was glad now that McKay had insisted they take a small tent. They had more grub than they would have been able to carry without the extra horse, too — potatoes from last year's crop and a big sack of good pemmican along with oats for the horses. McKay had been generous. Rob decided that he felt better about the trip.

As they rode the next day, they talked idly about many things — horse breaking, Mum's berry pie, what they would say to the North-West Mounted Police; but never what they would do if they didn't find them. Suddenly it occurred to Rob that he was doing nearly all the talking. Luke was only nodding and adding an occasional, "Yep or nope," before lapsing into silence. Rob realized that Luke had grown increasingly quiet for the past few weeks. Now he wondered why.

Rob had his answer later when, after a long silence, Luke suddenly blurted, "Rob, I think someday I should try to find my people."

Rob pulled his horse to a stop and stared at his brother. "We're your people, aren't we?"

Luke frowned. "Sure you are, but I need to know where my birth mother was going and why we were alone. I don't think that is the way of Indian folks. I think she was running away from somewhere."

Rob was silent, trying to remember. He was only six when, picking blueberries along the river with his mother, they had found the small boy crouched in the bushes beside the still body of a young Native woman. Her eyelids had fluttered when his mother bent over her, and she tried to speak, but failed. Dragging Rob by the hand, his mother had half-walked, half-run to the field where John was cutting hay with a scythe. Rob smiled inside as he remembered how Luke had taken his hand as they followed his father, who was carrying the sick woman, to the cabin. His mother had cared for her the best she could, but Luke's mother had only lasted two days more. That was the last time he ever saw Luke cry. The next day his father had pulled the canoe out of the woods and burned it.

Although his heart didn't agree, Rob nodded his head and said firmly, "All right, then when the time comes, I'll help."

Luke's smile lit up his face, but he said nothing.

"You're right as usual," Rob said later, after they had ridden several more miles. "The river's been turning east for the past couple of miles."

Luke grinned. "So in the morning we strike straight south. We're making good time, Rob."

CHAPTER THREE

By the time they stopped to rest their horses the next day, some of Rob's misgivings had returned, though he tried hard to force them away. There was nothing to shelter them and their horses from the burning July sun, except for an occasional outcropping from some of the low hills that appeared sporadically. The trees had disappeared with the river. Luke and Rob had filled their extra canteens to their tops before they left the river; but now they poured less water into their hats for the horses to drink, thinking it could be a long while before they would find water again.

Rob squinted into the sun, determined not to deviate from their ride straight south, even though they could have avoided the hill they were climbing now. They paused to let their mounts rest when they reached the top. Ahead there was only the undulating prairie broken by scrub cedar and sagebrush as far as the eye could see. Rob glanced over at Luke, and his spirit climbed a little as he heard the Native boy singing softly while sweat dripped into his eyes. Suddenly Luke stopped singing and, shading his eyes, pointed to a small cloud of dust rising in the south. "Think it's our herd?" Rob asked eagerly wishing he had a spyglass.

Luke waited several moments before he replied, "No, I can only make out three ... and they got riders."

Rob narrowed his eyes as he strained to see, and he felt his scalp prickle. "They're Indians."

Luke nodded without looking at his brother. "I'm pretty sure they're not Assiniboine."

There was no need to worry if the riders were Assiniboine, for that tribe often traded at Fort Ellice and sometimes camped near the river where the McCann's had their cabin. They had friends among them.

Without speaking, Rob and Luke turned their mounts down from the top of the hill, hoping they hadn't been spotted. "What do you think, Luke?" Rob asked. "They don't look like a war party — not that I ever saw one. Dad said Indians on the warpath wear paint."

"I guess so," Luke replied. "But they might try to take the pack horse, or maybe all our horses."

Rob felt goosebumps rising on his arms and his throat was dry. He eased his horse up the hill again, standing in the stirrups to catch another look at the approaching riders. "No sense taking a chance. We'll have to make a run for it and find the river again, even though it started to turn east." He looked up at the sun. "Remember the map showed after a few miles, the river made a little loop south again?"

Without waiting for a reply, he went on, "We'll be sure to find it if we head straight east. There'll be cover there. If they cut across our trail, they'd have a lot of trouble finding us in the trees." Rob knew his plan meant taking a big chance, but he couldn't think of any other way. The riders were sure to see where their horses had climbed the hill, and there was no use trying to hide without so much as big rock for cover.

"Let's go then," Luke said, grabbing the lead rope of the pack horse, and kicking his heels into Chris' flanks.

The pack horse was already tired from climbing the hill and tried to balk, but a whack with Rob's hat on her rear proved to be a strong incentive to move — and move she did. They raced across the open prairie, grateful to note the three riders weren't yet in view. *If we can't see them, for certain they can't see us*, thought Rob. When Luke slowed Chris and the pack horse to a trot, he followed suit.

About a half hour later he learned he had been wrong. Over the hoof beats of their own horses, Rob heard a thin, wavering call in the distance. Ahead of him, Luke turned to cry out, "They cut our trail!"

Afraid to run their mounts again so soon, they urged them into a steady lope. Beside Luke now, Rob shouted, "They were riding plenty fast. Their horses are likely more tired than ours."

"You think so?" Luke shouted and pointed over his shoulder.

Rob turned to look back and stared with disbelief. The three riders were in plain view and closing fast. "Let's go," he cried, slapping Sam with the ends of the reins. The three animals stretched their legs into a full gallop.

In spite of the pack horse, Luke soon pulled ahead. Rob's silent prayers were answered: a curving line of trees appeared in the distance.

Ahead of him by half a mile, Luke disappeared into the trees. Through the dust behind him, Rob could see that the riders were still far behind and a small feeling of elation began to calm his pounding heart. He whipped his tired mount into action. Bent almost double over Sam's neck, Rob felt the sweat pouring through her mane. "If we get out of this, I promise you oats twice a day…."

His whispered words ended when Sam stumbled to her knees and he flew over her head. There was only blackness then, and the last thing he heard was the rapidly approaching staccato of hoof beats.

Rob groaned softly when a moccasined foot pushed him over roughly. He opened his eyes. Luke had disappeared, and three young Native men stood looking down at him curiously. They were dressed in plain buckskins and wore no ornaments or feathers in their long, dark braids. Two of the men were lean and muscular, but the third was almost plump and seemed to be older than the other two. Dark eyes glittered from his pockmarked face as he stared down at the helpless boy. He spoke a language that Rob didn't understand, but the others laughed heartily.

One of the thin men strode over to Rob's mount where she stood, sweat streaming down her heaving sides. She didn't protest when he snatched up her dragging reins and examined her legs before leading her closer to where Rob lay. He sat up then, watching Sam walk and sighed with relief: she didn't appear to be injured. Nevertheless, it still wasn't a good situation. Even though there was nothing threatening in the his captors' manner, he knew that could change in an instant. He wondered where Luke was hiding.

Rob didn't have to wonder long. Glancing from Rob to the horse, the three men seemed to be arguing amiably, laughing as they spoke, until one halted abruptly and pointed to the trees beside the river. Rob turned his head to follow the pointing finger and saw Luke, stripped to the waist and barefoot, walking toward them.

Ignoring Rob, Luke raised his hand in a greeting and, hesitantly, the three Native men raised theirs. Their eyes looked puzzled as they stared at the approaching boy. When he halted one of them spoke, and Luke shook his head. Rob sensed that the man's words meant nothing to Luke. The men appeared to be asking questions, but again Luke clearly didn't understand. After a few failed attempts, the three men turned their backs on him and murmured among themselves.

Luke drew closer to Rob who growled, "Jings!, Luke, what're you doing here without your shirt and your rifle and where's the horses?"

Luke shook his head. "Later. You hurt?"

Rob felt his aching head. "Don't think so. Maybe I better try to stand up."

"Where's your rifle?" Luke asked looking around.

"I dunno." Rob peered at the Natives' horses and saw only blankets on the three backs. No place to put a rifle there, and the men each held only one. It was then he saw a glint of steel in a nearby patch of sagebrush. "Think I found mine."

At that moment, their three captors turned to the two boys. Through a series of pantomimes, Rob and

Luke began to understand that the men wanted to know where they could find Luke's horses. They seemed satisfied when Luke, in turn, gestured enough for them to understand that he had fallen off and lost them. The one with the scarred face pointed to the ground for Luke to sit, and then began to search the two bags hanging from Rob's saddle.

Rob couldn't remember for certain what his mother had packed in the bags; he was half-embarrassed as Scarface hooted with laughter while pulling out, one after another, the three pairs of socks Rob's mother had knitted during the winter. His laughter turned to shouts of glee when he yanked open the second bag and pulled out an oiled pack filled with dried meat. Rob was startled to see it. She usually only packed extra food for them to nibble on when they rode off on a hunting trip. The three men chewed hungrily on the meat and, to Rob's surprise, one of them came over to offer a strip to both Luke and him. Both boys shook their heads, and took care to smile. It would never do to make the men think they weren't appreciative of the gesture.

With a shrug, the plump Native yanked Rob to his feet, and with another gesture bid him mount Sam. Holding his breath, in fear that he may have misunderstood, Rob rose and took the reins that were held out to him. He clenched his jaw to hide the pain when both ribs and shoulders complained as he vaulted into the saddle, and he looked from Luke to the scarred Native, eyebrows raised in question. Laughing boisterously, the two thin men grasped Luke and tossed him onto the horse behind Rob.

"Wonder where they'll take us," Rob whispered over his shoulder, forcing himself not to show how scared he felt.

"Hope it's not far," Luke replied. "I'm getting cold."

The Native men leaped onto their horses and one of them slapped his reins hard on the rump of Rob's mount. She had been standing facing the trees and gave three giant leaps forward before she stopped. Rob and Luke turned their heads to see the men riding north. They were laughing loudly.

"Jings!" Rob said, blowing out his breath noisily. "We are ... we are ..." He shook his head, having no words to describe the relief he felt.

Luke slid to the ground. "You see the way they ate? I think they were just hungry."

Under his breath, Rob muttered a silent prayer of thanks. "Wish we had more in that bag, but I'd be far away from the truth if I said we should've told them where the rest is on the packhorse."

"If we knew more Indian words than a few Assiniboine,"

Luke said thoughtfully, "we might've figured out what tribe they're from."

"You remember some from your birth mother's language, though, don't you?" Rob asked as he followed Luke to the ground.

Luke gave a short laugh. "Just some — like for water and hungry — and that's only because Dad and Mum made me say them every day so I wouldn't forget."

As they talked they moved into the woods and across a shallow arm of the river. The two missing horses were standing in the water, drinking. "I thought they'd go deep in the trees," Luke explained, "so they couldn't be seen right off. I hid my rifle and took off my shirt so they'd see I wasn't just Indian coloured in the face."

Rob laughed and hugged his brother — something he rarely did. "Just wait till I tell Dad and Mum."

"Ah, wheesht," Luke said with a grin. "Go find your rifle."

When Rob returned with his weapon they began to plan. Torn between the need to rest the horses and the urge to move southward quickly, they compromised by leading their mounts through the shallow water for almost a mile before returning to the land on a rocky shore.

The two boys followed the river until the sun was high and then let the horses rest and nibble at the grass and moss under the mix of spruce and aspen trees. They ate the pemmican and the biscuits their mother made sparingly before stretching out in the leafy shade. In seconds they both were asleep.

CHAPTER FOUR

Rob woke with a start and reached over to shake Luke's arm. "Get up, Luke," he urged and looked up at the sky. "We slept too long. Half the day's passed."

Awake at once, Luke followed Rob to the horses and took the reins of the pack animal. "The river is turning east," he said to his brother.

Rob stared at the rushing water. "Seems to be," he said. He looked at the sky again and took a deep breath. "Guess then it's time to get away from these trees and head into the open."

Luke grinned cheerfully. "It's not as hot as it was anyway." He pointed north, at a thin line of grey clouds on the horizon. "If it rains a bit, it might be cooler tomorrow."

"Even if we lost some time by sleeping, we're making good time — and the horses are rested." Rob said, determined to be cheerful, too. "From the fort to the bend in the river only took us a bit more than a day, so it won't take more than that to get to where McKay said they're marking a boundary between us and the Yankees, and before that runs a good sized river."

Luke nodded. "And the Red Coats would be moving north of the boundary line. I'm thinking we'll meet up with them tomorrow."

Inspired by Luke's prediction, they decided to ride until it was too dark for the horses to see before they made camp.

The next morning they had begun to ride just as dawn was breaking. Even when the hot July sun reached its zenith and began its descent, without seeing even an antelope or a rabbit, Rob kept hoping Luke had been right. Their movements were casting long, wavering shadows as they rode. Sure that they would spend another night camped on the open prairie, Rob tried not to think about Luke's comment that he could smell rain. Besides, the line of grey clouds was still far behind.

The wind came suddenly and with it the rain, before they could hobble the horses and put up the tent. With the first bolt of lightning and explosion of thunder, the pack horse reared up and broke the line fastened to

Rob's saddle. While Chris behaved as she was trained to do, Sam whirled in circles and tried to flee the frightening noise. It took many long minutes for Rob to quiet the frightened animal. Wind-driven raindrops slammed into their faces as they looked through the rain for the pack horse. Luke shouted, "Over there!"

Rob thought his eyes were playing tricks on him: there wasn't one horse trotting in small circles, there were at least five. As Luke cried, "Its our herd!" Rob pulled hard on the reins and, with a determined effort, managed to turn his nervous mount to intercept the animals from one side while Luke moved to the other. Almost as though they were glad to be caught, the horses slowed as the boys approached. Speaking soothingly above the drumming of the rain on the hard-packed earth, they reached down to gather up the trailing bridle ropes. Rob leaned from his saddle to stroke each of the bobbing heads, losing sight of Luke for a moment. When he reappeared he was leading three more horses. "The rest of the herd must be around here," Luke shouted.

Rob whistled loudly hoping Smokey was nearby, and even though the stallion didn't appear, his heart was high. They would **find Smokey**, and his father was going to be mighty **happy when** they returned to the cabin.

Rob's **joy was short**-lived. When a flash of lightning turned night into day he felt a surge of dismay. These horses were tall with skinny legs and evenly clipped manes, unlike the ones they were seeking. The McCann horses weren't as high, but sturdy and bred to have muscular legs that wouldn't be troubled by long trail rides on the uneven prairie.

Rob and Luke stared at each other, disappointment on both of their faces. Finally, Luke said, "There's no post and no cabin near here, and these horses aren't wild. Somebody must be camped around here."

They spoke at the same time. "The police! The North-West Mounted Police!" The horses must have broken loose from their camp. Minutes later they were proven right. Two figures appeared ahead, lanterns swinging as their horses picked their way through the rain and darkness. Rob's heart lurched in his chest. What if they weren't the police, but the wolfers instead? There was nowhere to hide. He straightened his shoulders as the two riders approached more quickly. Not realizing he had been holding his breath, it came out with a whoosh; in the light of the lanterns, he saw small, round hats perched on the riders' heads. The wolfers had certainly not been wearing hats like that. He turned to Luke. "The police. We made it."

They were chilled to the bone and weary, but the grins on their faces were wide. Rob's relief was so great that he found it hard to speak, but Luke raised his voice above the sound of the storm, "I think we found something that belongs to you."

Holding his lantern high, one of the red-coated men shouted back, "That you did, for certain. Well done."

The second man moved closer and raised his lantern high. "Why, you're but a pair of lads. What are you doing out on this barren land and in a storm at night?"

"Looking for you," Rob blurted.

"And some horse thieves," Luke added.

"Then Constable McDuff and I are at your service," the first officer said. "I, being Inspector Denny — actually Sub-Inspector Denny of the North-West Mounted Police — F Troop."

Rob was awed. The rain had slowed, and the storm was moving eastward. A departing flash of light revealed the resplendent uniforms of the two men in their entirety. With one look he took in the black boots, red coat, and dark trousers, sodden now, but unlike anything he had seen before. Not sure how to address these men, he stumbled over his words. "Uh, thank you, uh, Sir."

Luke removed his low crowned felt hat to shake the water from it before he asked, "How far away are you camped?"

"Not far," Inspector Denny replied. "We're beside the Souris River. Do you know it?"

Never having been this far south before, both boys shook their heads. "I understand it is sometimes called Mouse River," Inspector Denny added.

More at ease now, Rob spoke up. "I heard tell of it. We must be near the boundary line then."

"Right you are," the officer agreed. "I fear McDuff and I will get little credit for returning with the horses when it is discovered two lads found them for us."

Luke and Rob stared down in amazement when they paused on the brow of a hill that had hidden the valley from them earlier in the day. Spread out as far as they could see were dozens of sputtering campfires, which the men below were trying to light now that the storm had passed; tents that had been half-mashed by the rain were being lifted from the mud. Most astonishing was a stream of more than fifty covered wagons, drawn by teams of oxen, that were being lined up side-by-side in groups of three amid a commotion of shouts and the cracking of whips. At least twice that many horse drawn carts were already parked, their wheels buried in mud up to the axles.

"Something to be grateful for," the inspector said, pointing toward the wagons. "Our men managed to get all of them here, in spite of those stubborn, lazy oxen."

"'Tis a blessing," Constable McDuff agreed.

All conversation ceased as, one-by-one, they allowed the horses to pick their way down the muddy incline to the valley below. Each of the officers took three of the runaway horses and Rob and Luke were free to manage their own. Even so, Sam was skittish and snorted excitedly each time she slipped a little. Rob relaxed after reaching fairly level ground near the end of the line of tents. His nose caught the drifting smell of roasting meat, and he realized how hungry he was.

"This is F Troop," Inspector Denny announced with a wave of his arm that seemed to indicate a group of wagons and carts, as well as four fires, surrounded by about fifty tents, as he lead the way to the picket line. When he and McDuff dismounted, Rob and Luke hastily followed suit and helped tie the horses.

Denny turned to Luke and Rob. "I think now might not be a good time to present you to the commissioner," he said thoughtfully. "Morning should do. Meanwhile, you are welcome to share our meat. For now, we have plenty. The water here is filled with fowl — ducks, prairie chickens, and others I don't recognize."

Excusing himself to go to the head of the line to make his report to the commissioner, Denny strode away; Constable McDuff gestured to a nearby campfire where a dozen or so men squatted. "I believe we may join these gentlemen," he said, "who no doubt will be happy to share their meal with the pair who saved their horses." He briefly explained how the boys had lost their herd, and then named each of the men by the fire. There were two Steeles, who were brothers, and two Gopsills, George and Alfred, who weren't, a Patterson, called Pat, and Leif Fitzroy Crozier, who held the rank of Inspector, head officer of F Troop. As the men continued to call out their names, Rob knew it would be useless to keep trying to memorize them now. He would work on that tomorrow.

The men rose in unison to greet Luke and Rob warmly. Their uniforms were spattered with mud and water dripped from their caps, but to Rob they appeared a happy lot. When he commented on this later, McDuff said, "Aye, they're that pleased that we are to rest here for a few days. There's long been time needed for the blacksmith to replace shoes on the horses and for this two-legged lot to wash clothes and themselves. 'Tis been a dusty business."

One of the Gopsills, a constable, had been looking from one boy to the other. "Are we to understand the pair of you be brothers?" he asked.

When both boys nodded, the man said wryly, "Sure you are."

Tired and hungry, Rob chose not to go into a lengthy explanation of how he happened to have a Native brother.

Instead, he picked up one of the tin plates lying on a flat rock and helped himself to a large chunk of meat. Luke had no reservations; he explained that he and his mother had been found by Rob's family.

His explanation was followed by words of sympathy from the men by the fire for the loss of his mother, and questions about where they had been going and why. Their interest was both genuine and friendly, which seemed to encourage Luke to keep talking. Not wanting to hear anything more about Luke's need to find his mother's family Rob interrupted: "How long have you been riding?"

"Ten days," McDuff replied.

On the other side of the fire, one of the men smiled ruefully and said, "And a very long ten days it has been, with one mishap after another."

Beside the man another laughed and clapped the speaker on the shoulder. "Pat, didn't your mum warn you this wilderness would be a far cry from your snug home in the city?"

"Oh, to be sure. But it was adventure I was hoping for; and I didn't expect the fighting to be against locusts, and mosquitoes so big and plentiful that they chewed the hide from me and me horse."

"Pay no attention to them, lads," McDuff said. "'Tis but the nature of men to be gloomy and complain when at rest, but when these have a job to do they do it well."

Inspector Crozier rose and tossed the remains of his tea to the ground. "I'm off to take another look at my horse. I have my doubts she'll be ready to ride with only a few days of rest."

Gopsill, who was the quartermaster, asked, "What's wrong with her?"

Crozier shook his head. "She came up lame just now as I rode in, and there's a bit of swelling. Doc Poett said he'll be by to look at her in the morning."

Rob surprised himself by blurting: "Could we come with you?"

Crozier appeared to be equally surprised, but he said, "Certainly. She's picketed near the river."

The dark brown mare whickered a greeting as Crozier approached, reached out a hand to scratch between her ears, and then bent to gently rub her left front leg just below her shoulder. To the boys, he said, "She's done all that I ask of her, though I don't think she was bred to this life."

Rob ran his hand down the animal's foreleg and stepped back for Luke to do the same. They looked at each other a moment before Rob asked, "How'd she come to have this swelling?"

"She was used to help pull one of the carts stuck in the mud," Crozier replied glumly.

Rob felt the leg again, slowly rubbing the large lump

he'd found. "What are you doing for her?"

Crozier shrugged. "Doc Poett gave me some liniment: I'm surprised you can't smell it." Then, with a hint of impatience, he asked, "Why do you ask?"

Before either boy could reply, Constable Patterson appeared and spoke to the inspector. "I'm told our fearless commander is expecting you at once."

Crozier muttered a few words under his breath before turning to the two boys. "I hope to return shortly," he said and strode briskly away.

Rob looked at Luke. "Do you think we dare?"

"She's hurting, isn't she?"

Both boys pulled off their shirts and trotted to the river to soak them in the water. They returned quickly and wrapped one of the shirts around the horse's leg. She flinched at the touch of the cold water and danced backward; but when Luke held her head firmly and spoke soothingly, she calmed and seemed to welcome the coolness of the cloth. When it warmed Rob stripped it from her and replaced it with the second shirt.

Rob forgot Constable Patterson was still there, and was startled when the man spoke. "I hope you're no' doing that which may harm her, else Inspector Crozier will have the three of us for breakfast."

Rob looked up quickly, relieved to see that the constable didn't really seem concerned. "It's what our dad does for our horses if they get lame," he responded. "We would have asked, but he left so fast."

"Well he might yet. Our Colonel French is a wee bit short-tempered these days."

Rob spoke hesitantly. "Uh, when we rode in we saw that your horses are...."

He paused to find an appropriate word.

Patterson finished for him. "A bit delicate?"

Rob nodded.

"'Tis plain, laddie, you know your horses. When you meet our fearless leader best not mention your thoughts to him. The colonel is a mite touchy on the subject."

Rob removed the now-warm shirt and, picking up the other one, ran back to the river to soak them again. When he returned he found that Constable Patterson had left and Inspector Crozier had returned. He was frowning as he gently rubbed the mare's foreleg. He looked up as Rob approached. "Luke here tells me cold is used for a swelling. I would have thought warmth would be best."

Rob bit his lip, searching for a tactful way to disagree. "I remember our dad telling us that swelling has heat and must be made cold, or it'll get worse. I don't know why, though." He looked at Luke for help.

Luke shrugged. "I just know it works."

Hands behind his back, Inspector Crozier stared at them for a long moment before he relaxed. "Carry on then, lads, and my thanks to you."

They alternated the cold, soaked shirts for the next hour before the swelling appeared to go down a little. Crozier had even taken a turn going to the river to wet the shirts. He shook hands with Rob and Luke. "I owe you my thanks and more. She's a fine animal, but I fear not meant for so rough a life."

The two boys returned to the campfire hoping to dry their shirts. A few of the men were still sitting beside it. "How is the mare then?" asked Constable Patterson.

"The swelling's gone done some," Rob replied.

One of the others called out from across the fire, "Maybe the colonel will hire you lads to aid our vet. With what we have to ride on this journey, he will be kept mighty busy."

There was a chorus of rueful chuckles. "You'll agree, though, 'tis a sight to behold as we parade across the prairie, each division on its own colour horse. And, for what — to impress the buffalo?"

A craggy faced trooper with greying hair had joined them, standing quietly with his back to the fire. In the silence that followed, he turned, raised his tin cup, and called out, "Aah what the devil does it matter at all, at all? Misery has an end, and after three days of naught but hardtack with our tea, we have birds aplenty, as well as a few days of rest. Take pleasure in what we have now, lads, and forget about what's behind us."

"Best you pay attention to what's behind yourself, John Bliss," called out Patterson. "You're britches are afire."

Steam was rising, from the warming of his wet clothes, but he jumped to action before he realized he wasn't on fire. The men broke out into uproarious laughter as he danced away into the night.

Inspector Denny interrupted the laughter, appearing from the darkness with a dark grey horse plodding behind him, its head drooping downward with each step. He grinned as he spoke to Rob and Luke. "It is our opportunity to return the favour." He held out the bridle rope of the pack horse they had lost. "She wandered here on her own."

The boys stammered their thanks. Denny directed them to an almost dry square of earth and advised them to put up their tent and get some sleep. Early in the morning they would be seeing Commissioner French.

CHAPTER FIVE

Colonel French wasn't at all what Rob had expected. As they walked up to the head of the line of tents they had asked Denny about the commanding officer. He told them the little he knew. The commissioner had trained in the British Royal Artillery then transferred to the Canadian Artillery. He held the rank of inspector when Prime Minister Macdonald expanded the police force and sent it west to keep the peace and arrest the whiskey smugglers. Prime Minister Macdonald was also the one who named the force the North-West Mounted Police.

Through a smoky haze rising from a clay bowl on the small table, Rob studied the officer as he and Luke waited inside his tent for him to finish writing. Rob wasn't sure what he had expected — a giant maybe, or at least someone with a commanding presence. In spite of his uniform appearing to be cleaner than any others, the square set of his shoulders, and the heavy black moustache, the colonel looked rather ordinary. When he put down his quill and closed the journal on his desk, he raised his head and stared at the boys with snapping dark eyes. There was something stiff and unapproachable in that look — hostile almost, as though he and Luke were on trial.

The man spoke pleasantly enough, though, and for a moment Rob relaxed. "I'm told we owe you thanks for the return of our horses." With a swift glance at Denny, who was standing beside the tent flap, he added, "We are grateful since, due to the carelessness of some of our men, we have none to spare."

Both Rob and Luke managed a small smile, and the officer went on: "The question is: what do we do with you now? Sub-Inspector Denny has spoken of your loss. After receiving a detailed description of your herd, we will keep watch for the thieves. It is our duty to bring a halt to all criminal activity in the region."

Rob swallowed hard before he spoke "Sir, Luke and I talked it over last night, and thought it best if we seek permission to follow along with you at least as far as Roche Percée. We'd know our horses if we see them, and the horse thieves, too."

The Commissioner stared at them for a long moment before favouring them with a thin smile. "Come now, we are on a serious mission. More serious I fear than finding a herd of farm horses." He brushed impatiently at the half dozen mosquitoes buzzing around his head. "Although it is doubtful your herd is ahead in this wilderness, as I said, if we see them, we will do our best to see they are returned to Fort Ellice and you will be notified. Meanwhile, we have a man sent down from there who is returning today, and he has agreed to allow you to travel with him."

Rob's heart sank. The herd hadn't been driven to Fort Ellice, and it hadn't been offered here for sale. The only other place he could think to search was way down across the border. There was no way he and Luke could get there: Inspector Denny had said there was talk of Sioux raids near the border. His mind worked swiftly, trying to come up with a plausible reason for them to stay with the police. It was Luke who spoke first.

"The mosquitoes are big here," he said, gesturing at the clay pot that was emitting thin trails of smoke. "Smoke doesn't keep them away."

"Now that's helpful," Rob said out of the corner of his mouth without taking his eyes off the commissioner. He wondered why Luke was talking about mosquitoes when he should be thinking of a way to keep from being sent home.

The officer, who was struggling to keep his dignity intact even while waving his arms at the bugs circling his head, snapped, "You are dismissed. The quartermaster will see you are supplied for your journey."

Determined to keep to their plan, Rob decided they would just have to tag along behind the wagons and oxen. He turned to follow Luke from the tent, then turned back quickly when the colonel called out, "Just a moment, please." He was standing now and looked at them curiously. "Why is it these infernal mosquitoes don't seem to be troubling you?"

When he saw Luke's smirk Rob almost laughed aloud, but to the officer he replied, "We rub some stuff on us that our mum makes. The skeeters don't like it."

Colonel French stared at them. "That is very interesting," he said slowly, emphasizing each syllable. "And do you have more of this concoction?"

"Some," Luke replied casually. "We don't need to carry much. We can make it anytime we find the stuff growing."

"Stuff? Stuff…" French said raising his voice. "What is it, and where can we find it?"

"Hard to tell. We don't know what it's called, but Rob and me know it when we see it."

Colonel French rose quickly. "Come with me. You will inform Dr. Kittson of this remedy. Everyone in the camp has suffered from those blasted creatures, even the horses."

As they followed the commissioner to a long tent nearby, Rob and Luke managed to whisper a plan.

Dr. Kittson was a big boned man with a full, greying moustache and serious, deep-set eyes. After the colonel quickly told him about the green daubs on the boys' faces and clothing, Dr. Kittson held out his hand to greet them while looking at Luke curiously. His comment was much the same as the ones they heard the night before. "Brothers, you say?"

Rob was pleased when the colonel interrupted, "Well, do you know what it is?"

The doctor reached over to take Luke's hat and rubbed one finger along the black band around the low crown. He then looked at the pale green streak on his finger, smelled it, and rubbed it together with his thumb before smelling it again. "It has a faint smell of mint," he said. He turned to Luke and asked, "Is this an Indian remedy?"

Luke shrugged. "I wouldn't know. Our mum gave a bit to us for the journey."

Colonel French asked impatiently. "Did she not once say what it is?"

Rob nodded. "Pennyroyal. She got the seeds from some cousins she has over in England." Certain now that the officer would take their bait, he added, "But there's another plant almost as good that grows on the prairie. Summertime we help Mum gather it. She boils it up and saves the water so that we have plenty for the summer and next spring as well."

"That's only for when we are home," Luke added. "We just carry the plant when we go away."

Eager now, the doctor started to leave the tent as he said, "May I see this plant?"

Rob quickly replied, "Sure enough, but it's all mushed up. That's so we can rub it on."

The commanding officer looked like he was about to explode. Taking a deep breath, he said, "Very well then. I order you to take some of our men and search this area for these plants."

Rob swallowed hard. "I don't know as if we would be able to find any around here — maybe there's more along the trail to Roche Percée."

Commissioner French's eyes narrowed, and he stared at Rob thoughtfully. Finally he said, "I see. Then let us agree to this: you may ride with F Troop until we reach Roche Percée, and in return, you will harvest all of this plant that can be found along the way."

As the two boys thanked the officer, they tried (and failed) to hide their grins.

The colonel stood, hands on hips, before his face cleared and he chuckled. "Dr. Kittson, I would appreciate it greatly if you wouldn't tell the rest of the camp how I have been bested by two lads." To Luke and Rob he said, "We have an agreement then, but you must promise to teach some of the men how to find this remedy before you leave us."

With a cheerful, "Yes, Sir, thank you, Sir," the boys left the tent.

"I gotta hand it to you, Luke. I never thought once of our mint stuff when he was swatting at the mosquitoes."

Luke shrugged. "We better find some in a hurry. Maybe the other side of the river, where the wagons haven't chewed up the land?"

"You go," Rob said. "I'll be along soon as I find Patrick Moss. If he hasn't already left for Fort Ellice, he can take word to our folks. He can tell them we're going as far as Roche Percée with the police and we'll ride back with Mr. McKay when he brings his horses down there."

CHAPTER SIX

After meeting with Patrick Moss, Rob saddled his horse and went in search of Luke. He found him kneeling on an open patch of ground above the river.

"Jings!" When he saw Rob coming, he gestured to a long hide sack beside him. It was bulging with green leaves. "There's enough of this growing here to let every one of the horses have a roll in it."

"I don't think that's what Colonel French had in mind." Rob knelt beside Luke and started to pick the leaves of catmint in front of him. "Hope they have more of these sacks."

Luke stopped working and leaned back on his heels. "Inspector Denny said we're going to be here three or four more days, right? Maybe we can dry a bunch of this in the sun, and everyone could carry some in his pocket."

Rob was doubtful. "Isn't it supposed to be wet when you rub it on?"

Rob suddenly found himself spread-eagled in the patch of mint, the ache of Luke's elbow in his side. "I guess you never heard of spit." Luke said.

Rob laughed and stood up, brushing away bits of leaves from his jacket and breeches, and succeeded only in decorating himself with more green streaks. "After we leave here, the troops might have trouble raising some spit. Patrick Moss said they're carrying some water barrels but no canteens."

Luke look startled. Rob nodded, "It's a fact. I haven't see any of the men drinking from a canteen: they go down to the river and dip in their cups. Colonel French must've figured on good water all the way."

"What about the horses and cattle?"

Rob shrugged. "They don't have canteens either, I guess."

"Then we're in trouble if there's a long stretch without good water. Our canteens sure don't hold enough for three hundred men and us."

"There won't be three hundred men," Rob replied. "Patrick told me that they're leaving eight men behind to look after the sick horses and the heavy stuff, like the mowing machines."

"Mowing machines?" Luke was aghast. "What are

they going to mow out here on the prairie?"

"That's what I asked. Patrick thinks they want to cut dry grass along the way, but mostly they're for later — after they build some forts and plant grain. The government figures on settlers coming out here someday."

Luke was thoughtful. "Mum would be happy about that. Don't know about the Indian camps, though."

"That's another thing Moss mentioned: some of the men that were marking the boundary line between the U. S. and Canada are on their way back east, and they said they shot at some Sioux who were trying to steal their horses."

Luke wasn't impressed. "Seems like every time a horse goes missing, Indians get blamed."

"I know that, but there's more. I didn't see them, but there's five big Métis sent from Winnipeg to be guides. They joined up a few days ago, and they told the colonel that there's been some Sioux raids on the Métis camps across the border that got people scared, and there's whole villages moving up to Canada."

Luke frowned thoughtfully. "Do you think the ones that caught us were Sioux?"

"I was thinking about that. I'm wondering if we ought to mention them to Inspector Denny."

The two boys looked at each other for a long moment and then shook their heads in tacit agreement.

The three Natives had been anything but warlike, and it was very possible it might seem like they were making up a story.

Rob sat back and looked at his brother, wishing he could make up his mind about what they were doing. Sometimes he was certain they would find their herd, and sometimes he wished they had returned to their cabin after they left Fort Ellice. Most of all, he wished he hadn't gotten Luke into this. Maybe Luke should go back.

Rob cleared his throat and said hesitantly, "Ah … uh … Roche Percée is a fair ride from here, Luke. Most likely it's safer riding with the police than if we rode back with Moss, but I think there's hard going ahead."

"So?"

"Well, for one thing, the horses keep playing out. Moss says they're eastern horses and don't take kindly to the rough prairie grass even if they can find it. They lost a bunch already and they're leaving some more behind here. If that keeps up, we might all be walking before we reach Roche Percée." Before Luke could say anything, he went on. "And it looks like they're running low on feed for the horses and the men, too. They haven't seen any antelope or buffalo to shoot for a long while."

"What about the cattle they're bringing? What're they for?"

"I guess they're to start a herd after the men settle somewhere, and besides all of them look too skinny to eat."

Luke looked levelly at Rob for a moment, then grinned. "So, if you're thinking of going back now with Moss, I'll come along. But if you're thinking of me going back alone, I'm not."

"Never crossed my mind," Rob fibbed and got to his feet. "Come on, this bag's full. Let's take it up to Dr. Kittson."

Word had spread through the camp that the two boys had something that might keep the mosquitoes from biting. They had to stop their horses twice to explain that the stuff wouldn't halt all the troublesome pests, but would help a lot. And they were right. In the following days, they heard that the men were finding fewer swelling bites on their faces and hands when they awoke in the morning. Rob and Luke were kept busy finding and drying more catmint. On the third morning they were especially happy with the report from Inspector Denny.

Rob and Luke found him perched on a rock in front of the morning campfire with his cup of tea and handful of hardtack. "Well, I am in the commander's good graces," he announced, "for bringing you here with your mosquito ammunition. Colonel French has been heard to say that these past two nights are the first he has slept through since we started this — ah — adventure, and he is even more delighted with the relief it has given the animals."

Recalling the remark Colonel French had made about tying horses, Rob guessed why Inspector Denny had been out of the colonel's graces, but he didn't want to ask.

"Although we have a free country," Inspector Denny said, "and a man should have the privilege of expressing his opinion, I made the mistake of commenting on the poor choice of saddles we have — never knowing our leader had done the choosing himself."

"Wheesht, man," said a voice from behind Rob. "'Twas not the complaining he took exception to. 'Twas three days past, when you spoiled his shot at the antelope by making such a commotion." He turned to find Constable McDuff behind him, cup in hand.

Expecting Denny to chastise the man under his command, Rob was relieved to see him grinning instead. "I've not forgotten that. I remind myself each day that I am fortunate not to have been shot in place of the antelope."

It was becoming more and more clear to Rob that Denny's men liked the officer and the informal way he treated them. Rob liked him, too; and felt a small surge of pleasure when Denny tossed away the rest of his tea and turned to Luke and him.

"Speaking of antelope, I except you lads have done your share of hunting. What do you say to the three of us riding out onto this prairie to look for some game?"

Rob spoke eagerly: "Just up above the river I saw some deer tracks. They must've come during the night else it would have been washed out by the rain."

"Capital!" the inspector said. "We can follow them and also look for antelope. I feel it is my duty to replace the one the colonel missed."

They followed the tracks of the deer into a thin strip of aspen and wild rose bushes that tore at their trousers, but they lost the tracks where the animals had crossed the river and couldn't find them on the other side. Picking their way carefully among the stones lining the water, they searched to see where the deer might have come ashore, but soon gave up for fear of one of the horses breaking a leg. They were some distance downstream when they emerged from the trees. Standing not twenty yards away was a slim antelope.

"I have him," Denny called even as the antelope bounded away. Yanking his rifle from its place, he kicked his horse with his heels, and it stretched its long legs and flew after the animal. Surprised by the speed of the officer's horse, Rob and Luke didn't even try to keep up with it, and settled for a gentle lope that left them behind.

"It won't be good if his horse steps in a hole," Luke commented. As he was speaking, they reached the top of a gentle slope from which they spotted the officer below, holding his rifle high as he struggled near the edge of one of the alkali sink-holes that dotted the prairie. Urging their horses into a gallop, Luke and Rob reached Denny just as he reached the edge of the muck. His horse, not more than three yards behind him, was wild-eyed and screaming in terror as she slowly sank into the sand and alkali.

"Help her," Denny cried as the boys pulled him to his feet. "Please, we have to help her."

"Try to calm her, Luke," Rob shouted as he leaped on his horse. "I'm going to get a rope." Bent low in his saddle, Rob urged his mount to go as fast as she could while trying to judge how far he was from the camp. It seemed to take forever, but it was only minutes before he saw someone in the distance riding to meet him. Galloping closer, he realized the erect figure and black bearded face was Colonel Macleod, second in command to Colonel French. And he was leading a horse.

Rob only had to utter a few words before both he and the officer were racing back to the sink-hole.

Rob breathed a sigh of relief when he saw that the head and neck of the horse were still free. But how to get her out? Denny had stripped off his jacket and trousers that were covered with sludge. Colonel Macleod snatched a rope looped from the horn on his saddle and swiftly turned it into a lasso. With one practiced swing, the rope settled around the trapped animal's neck, and the other end he quickly refastened to the saddle horn on his mount. Although strong hands helped the horse pull on the rope, they couldn't budge her.

Denny was beside himself with concern. "Ah, the poor creature," he muttered to himself. He spotted a second coil of rope the officer had dropped to the ground and, without warning, picked it up and launched himself into the air, landing flat beside his horse. Ignoring the cries of his companions, and clinging to the rope around her neck, with one hand he reached down through the ooze to force the rope around her front legs. He let go and, even as he began to sink, managed to tie the rope around her legs before throwing the other end to shore. Colonel Macleod held it high in the air as Denny used it to pull himself to Rob and Luke's outstretched hands.

After seeing Inspector Denny's efforts to free his horse, Rob had moved swiftly to unfasten the rope tied to the cantle of Colonel Macleod's animal and tie it to Luke's sturdy Chris. Rob looped it behind her front legs and around her chest — certain it would hold. He knew the tough little mare would pull with all her heart.

Rob was right. Head down and leg muscles bulging, she slowly dragged the squealing horse out of the muck.

CHAPTER SEVEN

Although he was coated with the grey and white goo himself, Inspector Denny stood beside his trembling horse, trying to rub the slimy coating from her sides and legs.

Standing with hands on hips, he observed the young officer. "Well now, Inspector Denny, it seems you've had another misadventure, and this time involved your uniform right down to your underwear." Macleod turned to Rob. "Do you know of a tub nearby that would serve to bathe the inspector and his animal?"

Both boys shook their heads, and the officer continued. "Then I fear it is the river, and the sooner the better else this may harden and we would have to leave him standing here as a warning to all who come by."

Despite the officer's joke, Denny's habitual grin didn't make an appearance. It was obvious that it was an effort for him to stand, much less walk. Still, he reached for the reins dangling from the mare's drooping head and said, "Thank you, Sir, for saving my horse." Turning to the boys, he added, "And to you young gentlemen as well. I fear I would have been in dire straits had you not been with me."

Rob wasn't sure how to respond to that, so he turned to the colonel and said, "It was fortunate that you happened along with a pair of ropes."

A momentary twinkle appeared in his deep set dark eyes as Colonel Macleod looked at Denny. "I always carry rope and an extra horse when I venture out for a bit of hunting. I am averse to sharing my saddle with an animal carcass when I am successful."

On their way back to camp, Denny astride Macleod's spare horse, the boys stopped at a sheltered bend in the river to help Denny wash his animal. She needed soothing words of persuasion to step into the water, but when she felt solid earth under the surface, she lay down and allowed herself to be rinsed of the white mud. When man, animal, and uniform were clean they proceeded into the camp.

Rob expected a score of questions when Denny's men saw him ride into camp dripping wet and in his underwear, but saw only raised eyebrows and shaking heads. Apparently they were accustomed to events like these involving their officer. On the ride back into camp Denny had explained that Colonel Macleod's remark had been in reference to the night Denny thought one of his men was missing and ordered the cannon fired. This had frightened the horses, and they spent half the night rounding up the forty that had bolted. The worst of it was: the missing man was already fast asleep in his tent.

In their own tent that night, Luke fell asleep quickly, but Rob lay awake wondering if Inspector Denny would be in deep trouble for the condition of his horse. Colonel Macleod had sent the veterinarian down to look at her, who made it plain that she couldn't be ridden for some time.

In the morning, however, Denny appeared unworried when he joined them for breakfast after his usual meeting with Colonel French and the rest of the officers. Rob noticed that the young officer now was mounted on a dun coloured horse, and his saddle appeared to have been cleaned and polished. Denny must have been up all night.

"We'll be moving out today," Denny announced. He poured cups of tea for Constable McDuff and himself, and reached for a half-baked round of bread. "Best start to pack up as soon as you're able."

McDuff had been peering upward over the rim of his cup as he drank. Lowering it, he looked worried as he spoke. "I fear for the horses that must pull carts half buried in mud these past days. And more for those that are hitched to the cannon. We had trouble enough pulling guns weighing a ton into this valley. Tell me how they can be expected to get them to the top of hills that are wet with the rain still."

Denny's smile was gone, and his voice was deadly serious; he looked at each of the men sitting around the fire in turn. "It won't be easy. We can but try, and when we do I want you to remember this. Though we must take care not to lose more horses, it is more important that we take care not lose any man among us. Take care. That's an order."

Rob, too, had wondered how all those heavy wagons would get out of the valley, and he was very uneasy. He had heard the men in F Troop talking and knew that quite a few of them were half-sick from eating too much fresh meat while they camped. And now they were called on to do a very tough job. From the frown on Luke's usually impassive face, he sensed that his brother shared his feeling.

They were right to worry. In an effort to criss-cross the steep hillside rather than drive the horses and oxen straight up, cart drivers from C Troop pulled in front of the oxen-driven wagons of F Troop doing the same. Pandemonium! A wagon and a half dozen carts and their contents tumbled downward. None of the Métis drivers were injured; but tempers flared as drivers shouted accusations over the screams of the frightened horses. Colonel Macleod's voice rose above the rest. His horse was nervously dancing around on uncertain footing, but his voice was calm. Macleod ordered them to unhook their horses and rescue what goods they could. Then, dismounting, he led his horse to the very bottom of the slope, where a team of six horses and their riders were beginning the arduous task of pulling the cannon up the hill.

Inspector Crozier had ordered the boys to keep clear of the men, and from their vantage point on top of the hill, Rob and Luke watched the six thin, long-legged horses strain as they leaned forward in their harness. "They won't make it," Luke muttered.

Crozier and Denny, riding on either side of the lead team, were calling out encouragement as they leaned to grasp the bridles of the struggling horses. Oxen, hitched to the wagons below, waited their turn. All was eerily quiet, except for the harsh breathing of the three teams straining forward; slowly, inch-by-inch, the first of the big guns moved upward. Rob found himself leaning forward in his saddle as though trying to help the animals. The bottom of the hill was the steepest of the climb, forcing the horses to bend their front legs, to dig in with their hoofs, then put a terrible strain on their knees as they were straightened for the next step. Rob watched, his throat dry.

He had just begun to relax when the cannon reached the point where the slope was more gradual when, without warning, two of the lead horses fell to their knees. The cannon came to a halt. Shouting men quickly ran to put blocks behind the carriage to keep it from rolling backward, while others removed the harness from the two horses. The veterinarian and Colonel French reached them at the same time, and after a long examination, the vet rose and shook his head. Colonel French rose stiffly. Head up and body erect, he climbed up to his waiting horse, standing not far from Rob and Luke. As he passed by, Rob thought he heard the officer mutter, "God forgive me." He looked at Luke to see if he had heard, but his brother was watching the scene below.

A team of six oxen had been taken from a wagon below. It was plain they were meant to replace the two horses, which had been dragged to the side.

"Maybe they should have tried them in the first place," Rob said.

Luke was staring at the two horses lying as though dead. "They had no strength left, only heart."

The driver of the wagon the oxen had been taken from was waving his arms and protesting loudly. Rob liked the Métis drivers who sang and made jokes while they cared for their oxen. He had enjoyed their friendly teasing about the smaller horses he and Luke rode, and he had made a few barbed remarks regarding oxen in return. Now he sympathized with the driver's concern for his team, for they might be able to help pull up the cannon, but would they be able to pull his wagon after? Colonel Macleod calmed the man, who finally stalked off to sit on a rock.

The oxen certainly made a difference in hauling the cannons up the hill, but it still took more than two hours to get both of them to the top. Meanwhile, more of the horses pulling carts had slowly made their way up, followed by the oxen-pulled wagons. Police on horse back rode on either side of the teams of oxen hitched to each wagon until all of them reached the summit. Only the wagon without a team remained below with its disgruntled driver. Inspector Denny went from one team to another all standing with their heads down, breathing heavily.

"They should rest for some time before any of them are made to pull up the last wagon," he reported to the colonel.

"Nonsense," Colonel French snapped. "They have been resting for four days. These drivers claimed their animals have double the endurance and strength of a horse. Let them prove that."

Rob thought they would use one of the team of oxen that had pulled a wagon, but it was the team that had pulled the cannon that was unhitched and turned back to the hill. When they reached the edge the oxen stubbornly refused to go a step further. They flinched with each crack of the whip, but wouldn't budge. Finally Inspector Denny ordered them to stop, and turned to Colonel Macleod. "Sir, there is not a beast here that has the stamina to climb the hill again, even without a wagon. I believe the only choice we have is to abandon the wagon."

Colonel French rode closer. "You are possibly right, Inspector. What is in the wagon?"

"It isn't heavily loaded," Denny replied. "One team of oxen could do it. It's the wood and the food and F Troop's personal goods."

"I see," Colonel French said. "Then since the goods are for the comfort of your men, I suggest we leave the wagon and they go down and bring up what they can carry. They can stow it with another troop."

Denny's face turned red, and Rob was afraid he was going to explode with anger. His men worked hard, without complaining. They deserved better than to labour like animals in this heat.

Before Denny could protest, Colonel Macleod said softly, "If you will excuse me, Colonel, I would like to make a suggestion."

The short discussion was in voices so low that Rob couldn't hear. When Colonel French rode back to the shade of the only two trees on the hill, Colonel Macleod announced that F Troop would wait until the oxen were rested enough to retrieve the wagon while the rest of the train went on toward Roche Percée. Rob had another thought, and it caused his scalp to prickle: he and Luke were supposed to ride with Denny's F Troop, and this meant that they would be hours behind the main body all the way to Roche Percée and there were supposed to be hostile Sioux somewhere around. Suddenly Luke urged his horse closer to Rob and whispered a question.

Rob was startled, but thought about it for a moment. It might work. With a jerk of his head he signalled for his brother to follow him and went over to Colonel Macleod who was talking to Denny. "Excuse me, Sir," Rob said. "Luke and me, well we kind of would like to try to get that wagon up here."

The eyebrows of the two men shot upward in unison. Before they could respond, Luke said, "My horse was bred to do more than carry a rider. She can pull a big load of hay all by herself uphill or down."

"We aren't sure about mine," Rob confessed. "She's not been trained to pull any kind of load, but she's one of ours, so we probably would do fine."

Both officers were doubtful, but after several minutes of discussion, agreed the boys could try — providing they didn't damage their animals.

"Damage our animals?" Luke scoffed as they led their horses down the hill, the heavy traces of the harness trailing behind. "As if we don't know better."

Rob's confidence began to shrink when they reached the wagon and started to hook up their horses. Close up, it looked bigger than he had thought. They'd been giving their mounts a handful of oats each day from the small supply their pack horse had carried, but they'd run out after reaching the Police camp. Even without oats he was sure they were just plain tougher than the horses from the East.

Rob muttered a small prayer under his breath asking that they be strong enough for this job. He stripped off his saddle and threw it into the wagon. Then he rubbed the mare vigorously with the saddle blanket and tossed it into the wagon as well. Running his hand down Sam's long, grey and white nose, Rob whispered words of praise in her ear. He and Luke looked at each other, nodded, and slapped each horse on her rump. In unison, the two horses threw themselves into their harness and the wagon lurched forward. The beginning of the slope was so steep that the two animals looked like they were climbing a staircase: a long jerk forward followed by a short pause.

Instead of following the rutted paths made by the preceding wagons, Rob and Luke moved up the slope at a much longer diagonal, which made the high covered wagon lean precariously. The watching troopers were dead quiet. Clutching Sam's bridle, Rob walked beside her, matching her steps. As the climb grew steeper their progress slowed, but held steady; Rob's heart beat faster with pride. Even when their hoofs slipped or they dislodged stones or found a patch of soaked earth, Chris and Sam only arched their necks and pulled harder. Tough and tenacious, boys, horses, and wagon reached the gentler rise and then crested the top edge of the valley far away from the rest of the wagons. The crowd of watching men cheered loudly.

The horses were sweating, but scarcely more than Luke and Rob as they quickly removed the harness before anyone got the idea that their horses should pull the wagon to the next stop. They turned when they heard a voice calling. It was Colonel French. "I would like a word with you," he said. He was followed by a trooper neither boy had seen before.

CHAPTER EIGHT

When he reached the two boys Colonel French pulled his horse to a stop and stared down at them. "Yes, well, ah, well done, lads." He paused, then went on. "I've a question. Are the horses you are searching for," he gestured toward Sam and Chris, "of the same breed as these?"

"Yes, Sir," Luke replied. "Our pack horse might be, too. It came from Fort Ellice, and our dad's been selling them one or two every year."

"This year was our big year," Rob said, trying not to look as bad as he felt when he thought about the herd they lost. "But the wolfers took most of them."

The officer dismounted and ran his hands along the withers and each of Chris's legs. He said nothing, other than "Hmmm," before he swung back on his horse and loped over to where Colonel Macleod and Denny were organizing the wagons and carts into a line for the journey onward. Rob and Luke followed him with their eyes for a few moments, and then turned to each other, both faces wearing a perplexed look. The trooper who had followed the colonel was still seated on his horse nearby, chuckling.

"He's a hard one to understand, is our Commissioner French." He swung off his horse and offered his hand to Luke then Rob. "Name's Fred Bagley," he said. "What's yours?"

Rob eyed the trooper swiftly while he and Luke introduced themselves. He noticed a shiny instrument tied to the pommel of the trooper's saddle. *Jings! He must be the company bugler. But he doesn't look a bit older'n me — maybe not as old.* Realizing he might have been staring, Rob hastened to say, "You must be the bugler. We both like hearing it."

Luke had no worries about tact. "How old are you?"

Bagley's eyes twinkled. "No sense pretending I'm older'n I am when it's plain I don't shave yet, is it? I'm fifteen."

"Didn't you have trouble joining up?" Rob asked. "I heard you're supposed to be at least eighteen."

"That's right, but I wanted to join up something fierce. My pa has some friends that were doing the recruiting and they figured out a way."

Rob and Luke waited for Bagley to explain more, but instead he said, "I heard about why you're here. You're looking for your horses, right?" Rob nodded. "Well, the pair you're riding are something special. I never saw a team that could pull a load uphill like that."

"Our dad's been breeding horses a long while," he said. "He doesn't sell them until they're good at pulling and riding both." Rob felt more comfortable with the young trooper all the time. It was the first time he had met someone his own age other than the friendly young Natives who lived near their cabin, but it was hard to talk with them. Some spoke a few words of English, but Rob and Luke spoke hardly any Assiniboine.

"Inspector Denny said the stallion is supposed to be grey with a silver mane and tail."

Luke broke in. "He's not just supposed to be. He is."

"Right," Bagley said hastily. "I didn't mean to sound like I didn't believe that. I sure don't blame you for trying to find him. But is it true you're going back home in a few days?"

Before either could respond, they heard a shout in the distance and Bagley smiled. "It's my turn to drive a wagon, I guess I have to go, but I'll look for you when we camp."

* * *

Rob didn't know whether to be sad or glad when he heard Colonel Macleod say that the Métis guides thought it would take about four days to reach Roche Percée. *I'll be glad to get home so I don't have to worry every day that Dad could have been hurt worse than Mum thought. Who'd take care of the horses and cut the hay? Mum will try, but she's just not strong enough for all the chores. Besides she's got plenty to do taking care of the chickens and garden and the cabin and Dad. I wish we could bring some good news, like finding some sign of the herd.*

The trail to Roche Percée took longer than the guides thought it would — seven days of dry, hot, dusty riding and walking. To save the exhausted horses, the colonel ordered that the troops dismount and walk every other hour; Rob felt the soles of his boots wearing thin on the stony soil. To add to the general feeling of misery, rations had been cut twice. Rob and Luke had finished their food and oats and given the pack horse to a trooper to ride. At night they camped near thin streams, fouled and muddied by herds of buffalo that passed through as they migrated. Some of the horses became so thin and weak that five men were assigned to fall behind and bring them along more slowly. Rob felt a surge of relief when he saw the huge rock with a wide hole in the centre. Bagley had been told that there would be good water nearby and grass for the horses, and there was no denying that both Chris and Sam's ribs showed plainly under their hides.

By the time Rob and Luke saw the rock, the first of the line of horses and wagons had long since passed it and were camped about four miles beyond among a mix of poplar and aspen trees growing near a stream of fresh water. They had chosen to ride at the end of the line where Colonel Macleod spent most his time with the F Troop and worked as hard as any trooper to keep the straggling cattle, spare horses, and the occasional wagon from falling too far behind. The colonel would sometimes order two or three of his men to stay back with him to allow the most exhausted of the animals to rest for a little while. Rob and Luke would stay, too. Thus they came to know the soft spoken colonel much better than the rest of the officers — with the exception of high spirited Inspector Denny.

For Rob, Colonel Macleod seemed like the heroes in books Mum had Luke and him read last winter. Because of what he had seen and heard four nights ago, Rob also knew that the colonel stood up for what was right.

Luke and he had been watering their horses not far from a tent where Colonel French was apparently working himself up to an exploding point. "A minor issue you say!" they heard him shout. "Then, Sir, I must question whether or not you think the way an officer should."

A murmured response followed, but the two boys couldn't make out the words. They could hear Colonel French, though. "I repeat: during the night a slab of bread that had been baked for today's ride disappeared. The thief must have been one of the night guards. I put it to you, Colonel Macleod, to find which of them is guilty."

A murmured question was followed by: "He will be clapped in irons of course!"

Luke and Rob looked at each other, eyes wide with disbelief. In irons over a slab of bread! The next moment, they heard Colonel Macleod raise his voice. "Colonel French, we both signed the Articles of the North-West Mounted Police: no man can be punished before he has a trial to defend himself. Given the hardships these men have borne and will bear, I suggest that a trial over losing a slab of bread would be a waste of time and lower their morale considerably." There was a pause. "Unless, of course, it would amuse them for days to come."

That seemed to quiet the commanding officer, and they saw Colonel Macleod leave the tent. No guard was put in irons.

Rob knew that Luke and Bagley admired the officer too; they had talked about him a few times while they camped. Once, while they had been lying in the shade of one of the wagons, Luke said to Bagley, "He reminds me of my dad."

"Dad!" Rob yelped, thinking of his big, burly, red-headed, explosive father. Colonel Macleod was almost the opposite with his thin frame, high-cheeked face, and dark eyes. True, he also wore a full beard and moustache but his were black as could be. But maybe Luke was right in a way. In spite of his quiet voice, the troops seemed to be respectful of his authority just as it was plain the men at Fort Ellice respected Dad.

Rob turned to Bagley. "I guess I know what Luke means, but Dad came over to be a farmer and raise horses, and the colonel came over when he was just a youngster, and he went to a university and got to be a lawyer."

Bagley nodded, and added, "Then he joined the militia — the one that put down that uprising at Red River." He put his hands behind his head and looked up at the sky. "Good thing he's along with us: He's good at keeping Colonel French from blowing up in little pieces."

"You mean when he found out a slab of bread was missing?" Luke asked.

"Well that and a couple of other times. We no more than got started when Colonel French got in a real dander over the horses."

Horses! All attention now, both Luke and Rob sat up to listen.

"First you gotta know what happened at Fort Dufferin before we even left. It was late at night, and everybody was asleep except the guards, when all of sudden the worst thunderstorm I ever saw hit the camp. It was like the worst nightmare you ever had. First came the wind and the rain and then big hail stones that knocked down the tents. We had two hundred horses picketed, and most of them tore loose and ran through the camp like they'd gone crazy. Some of the men got hurt. I tell you it was pure hell, but even half-undressed, the officers and men acted like it was just any other day. They caught the horses that they could and tied them, but almost a hundred ran off."

Luke and Rob were wide-eyed hoping for more, and Bagley didn't disappoint. "There's five men here I can tell you that I admire almost as much as Colonel Macleod, and that's Oliver, Barton, Sinclair, Wilde, and Francis. With all that lightning and rain, they jumped on any horse they could catch and rode bareback after the ones that got away."

"Whew!" Rob said under his breath. "Did they find them?"

Bagley shook his head. "Nope, too dark. They came back after a long while. In the morning more than fifty men were sent to look. They found most of them — all except about twenty-five."

"Was that when Colonel French got himself in a ..." Rob began.

"No," Bagley interrupted. "Matter of fact, next morning he even said, 'Well done, men.' They deserved it. With the sun up, the ones that didn't go after the horses hustled around and got the camp back up and running, and laughing while they did. But the fuss was about horses. We had two more inspectors that came a day or two later. They were supposed to be in charge of the horses, and they nearly threw fits when they got a look at the ones the colonel had picked for us. Right in front of the whole camp they told him off. They said the horses were for parades and parties — not for pulling anything or for riding over rough land. They claimed they wouldn't last more'n a month."

"What happened?" Luke asked.

"About what you'd expect. There was a big shouting match that ended with the two inspectors stomping away to their tents and packing up to leave."

Rob frowned. "What'd the colonel do?" he asked.

"Nothing he could do," Bagley replied. "His face was redder'n his jacket, but he marched like a soldier back to his tent. Colonel Macleod followed him, and when they came out, Colonel French's face wasn't red anymore."

"I guess it must be hard to be responsible for men and horses and supplies and maybe Indian attacks, and...."

The sound of Colonel Macleod's voice ended Rob's musings. He rode closer and said, "If the chief trader from Fort Ellice does meet us at here with horses as planned, I understand that is where the pair of you leave our company. I expect you'll be pleased to get home — your mother and father as well."

"I expect so," Rob replied.

Luke spoke up. "Mum will be pretty happy, but Dad's probably going to give us an earful."

He had never once punished either of them with the strap, but Rob wondered if this time might be Dad's first. He had never wished so hard for anything as he wished that they could bring Smokey and the herd home.

The colonel turned his horse to ride ahead with the report, calling back a simple, "You'll be missed," as he went.

"At least you won't be going to Fort Ellice just with the riders who are bringing the horses," Bagley said later when the three boys pitched their tents. "I heard that Colonel French is having Inspector Jarvis take some of the sick men, cattle, and horses up to Fort Ellice. After they rest up, they're all supposed to go way up north to one of the Hudson's Bay forts."

"Which one?" Luke asked. "Fort Carlton?"

"No, way north — Fort Edmonton."

Rob stared at Bagley. "That's a fair way to go even when you're in good shape. How're they going to get there with sick men and sick horses?"

"That's what I asked Inspector Walsh. He said some of the men think the colonel's just trying to make it easier to get to Fort Whoop-Up and back home before winter; but Walsh said he's doing what's right. They don't know what they might run into or what kind of country, and it would be hard on any that are sick."

Bagley bent to spread out his bedroll. "Besides," he went on, "Walsh said Jarvis is going to be in charge, and Sergeant-Major Sam Steele is going along to help. He said that they're the best, and if he had to pick someone to get the sick men to Fort Edmonton, they're the ones he'd pick."

"I guess we'll find out," Luke said slowly. Rob knew his brother was dreading going home empty handed.

Although it was late July, the nights were cool, and both Rob and Luke forgot some of the hardships of the journey as they slept soundly in their tents after washing up in the narrow river. It felt good to be clean, but their clothes had become so worn they didn't dare scrub them. *Besides seeing Mum and Dad and eating some good food*, thought Rob, *it'll be good to change these britches*. He would miss these men, though — especially Inspector Denny. There'd never been anybody as full of fun as Denny. He had been quieter these past two nights, since Colonel French caught him dancing and singing around the campfire with the Métis drivers again. The colonel had berated him in front of the men for behaving in a manner unbecoming to an officer. Rob figured that didn't earn the colonel a lick more of respect from the men.

In the early morning, Luke stopped rubbing down his horse and looked at the grey sky turning pink. "I think I'll be happy to get home," he said to Rob.

Rob understood. The air was fresh and cool before the sun was up, and, for the moment, it was quiet — the men weren't yet busy around the camp, stirring up the dust. It felt like the mornings when they went out to feed the horses before running back to the cabin for breakfast. If only they weren't returning to the cabin empty-handed this time.

Both boys turned with a start as they heard a commotion: McDuff had a firm grip on the bridle of a dispirited looking horse. Its wild-eyed rider was waving his arms and demanding to see the colonel. "Wheesht, man," McDuff shouted back. "Get down and wait. 'Tis likely the colonel isn't yet awake."

When the stranger dismounted Rob noticed he wasn't very tall — not much taller than the old flintlock he carried. While the two men were talking, Rob felt himself wrinkling his nose in disgust. He glanced around quickly, hoping no one had noticed. He studied the man. *It's not that his clothes are so dirty and tattered — mine aren't much better. I guess it's the knotted-up black beard and the way his eyes keep shifting around the camp when he's talking.*

McDuff gestured for the stranger to take a seat on a rock near the fire. By way of introduction, he said, "Name's Morrow. Hunter and guide, I am."

Rob backed his horse away, but was still within earshot.

"Hear you're figurin' on goin' up to Fort Whoop-Up," the dark man said, taking the cup of tea McDuff offered. "Got a ways to go, aintcha?"

McDuff nodded and Morrow went on, "Better turn north if you plan on findin' it."

Rob couldn't help himself and went to join them. "Have you been there?"

Morrow turned to stare at Rob for a moment before he answered. "For sure," he said. "But I ain't no whiskey trader."

McDuff was interested now. "Wait here," he said and strode off.

Rob and Luke were left alone with the stranger. The trapper looked at Luke and Rob in turn. Finally he said, "You're a mite young for a policeman."

Something about the man made Rob reluctant to tell him the full story, but Luke apparently didn't share his reservations. "My brother and I were captured by Indians when we were little," he said, casting his eyes down sadly.

"That so," Morrow replied. He had a slight frown above his narrow black eyes, which were still darting around the camp.

Rob hid his grin as Luke nodded slowly. "It took us years to get away. We ran into the police a long way back, and they're taking us back to our tribe."

A sneer appeared on Morrow's face. "And what tribe would that be?" he asked. "Ain't never seed a red-head Injun."

Before Luke could decide which tribe they were from, McDuff returned with Colonel Macleod and Inspector Denny. The colonel looked down at the man and asked, "Why do you wish to see Colonel French?"

"That the one leading this outfit?" Morrow said without rising.

"That's right."

Morrow replied slowly, "I expect I can do him and the rest of you a service — for a price."

Colonel Macleod got right to the point. "I take it you've been told where we are heading and you wish to show us the way?"

Morrow's face wore a sly look. "Met up with some of them boundary-making men. Told me you're lookin' for the meetin' of the Bow and Belly. You want them that sells whiskey to the tribes."

The colonel nodded, and Morrow went on. "I been lookin' around here. Same men got somethin' else you need."

Col. Macleod was getting impatient. "And what is that?"

"I see your horses are looking wore out."

McDuff snapped, "And how would this be of concern to the likes of you?"

"Maybe nuthin'. Maybe sumpin'. I know where to find a herd of about a dozen or more — led by a fine lookin' stallion — fit for the lead man of an outfit like this. Ain't never seen nothin' like him."

"Come with me." Macleod said to Morrow, then turned to McDuff. "Have his horse looked after."

CHAPTER NINE

For a split second, a shocked Rob and Luke stood rooted to the spot before starting after Colonel Macleod and Morrow, their faces eager and mouths open to speak. The colonel turned to them and ordered in a low tone, "Not a word. Not one single word."

Dumbfounded, Rob and Luke looked at each other: didn't the colonel realize that he had to be talking about their horses? It didn't occur to them to disobey, but they followed behind the two men as they walked through the trees until they reached Colonel French's tent. Colonel Macleod went in alone for about five minutes before signalling for Morrow to enter. Waiting outside with Luke was the hardest thing Rob had ever had to do. He wanted to rush in and demand to know where Morrow saw the horses and which way they were going.

Followed by his brother he crept closer to the open flap of the tent.

From inside they heard Colonel Macleod relating the Métis' desire to sign on as a guide. "Mr. Morrow also believes he knows where we can buy some horses."

"Whose horses are these?" Colonel French inquired. "My impression is that the Indians do not part easily with their animals."

"Not Indians — white men — maybe whiskey traders."

"How do you know that?" the officer asked sharply.

Suddenly defensive, Morrow said, "If they are bad men, me, I didn't know. I only helped drive horses south — south to their camp in the Sweet Grass Hills. From there, I came here." He hesitated a moment, then added, "They wanted to sell them to the men who mark the boundary, but they were gone. Maybe now they'll go to Fort Benton."

Rob's heart sank, and he thought he saw tears in Luke's eyes. If the horses were driven to Benton, they would probably be sent on one of those steamers to be sold far south of the border. He put his arm around his brother's shoulders and turned away. They both stopped short when they heard the colonel say: "Well, Colonel Macleod, since we must ride to Fort Benton in a few days anyhow, perhaps we should take the time to look at these horses if they are still there."

Without waiting to learn if the Métis had been hired as a guide the boys stumbled back to the campsite. Rob's spirits shot up before falling back down. It was exciting to know someone had seen the herd, and the police might get to them soon. But that must have been days ago. Where might they be by now?

Luke spoke almost angrily, "Even if we try to go ahead of Inspector Jarvis to Fort Ellice and ride hard, it'd take three days, and maybe four or five more for Dad to ride down and catch up with the troop. All our horses would probably be gone by then. Smokey'd be the first to go."

Rob had a spark of hope and an idea. "Let's ask Colonel Macleod if we can go on with them and down to Fort Benton. He doesn't have to let Colonel French know. We could make ourselves scarce when he's around."

"Sure! But even if we find our herd, how would we get them back from Fort Benton. It's a long way, isn't it?"

Rob bit his lip. Hard. "I've been thinking about that. Maybe we could hire one of the drivers to help us get the herd back."

"With what? We don't have any money."

"We could promise him a horse — one of the best. And, maybe, um, we could ..." Rob's thoughts died.

Luke was still hopeful. "Let's see how far it is. We can ask Colonel Macleod when he comes back."

When he returned, the colonel made a point of searching them out, beckoning them to a private spot beyond the tents. "Not appearing to being the most trustworthy sort, I thought it best that Morrow not know that you are seeking your herd, and the colonel agreed."

"Did he hire Morrow as a guide?" Rob asked, and the officer nodded.

"He thought about it for some time, but in the end he did. The guides that we have now admit they don't know the land ahead. Not only that — they don't speak the Blackfoot tongue, and this Morrow does. Or says he does."

"Colonel Macleod," Luke blurted, "how far would it be to Fort Benton from right here?"

The officer looked at him sharply. "Lad, if you two have any thoughts of riding on to Fort Benton on your own to look for your herd, you best put them aside. I'm told it is a very rough place, and riding down to it alone would be very dangerous."

"It's just a town, isn't it?" Rob argued.

"Having never been there, I cannot say what it is. I understand it was first a fort for trading and now has an American army post with a few men to watch for whiskey traders. However, it is the last northern stop on the Missouri River, and most of the buffalo hides and furs are taken there to be sold. It's bound to be, as I said, a very rough place."

"But maybe our horses are down there," Rob said. "Do you think we could keep on riding with you down to Fort Benton?"

"Now then, lad," Colonel Macleod admonished. "The colonel has more than once made a point of seeing that you return to Fort Ellice."

Rob felt defeated. With his last faint hope, he went on, "When you get there, then, will you keep watch for our herd?"

"And arrest the outlaws that took them and bring back the horses?" Luke asked with sudden eagerness. "You could keep them and pay Dad after while — not Smokey, though."

Although Colonel Macleod seemed sympathetic, he said, "I cannot promise such a thing, Luke, much as I'd like to. We have no authority south of the border. To add to that, neither Colonel French nor I have ever seen your horses, so how are we to claim them and brand those who have them as outlaws?"

Rob seized on Luke's idea. "That's just why we should go with you. We know our horses."

"As I already told you, Colonel French has made certain you will leave with the men who are bringing horses down from Fort Ellice and Inspector Jarvis. I can promise he won't change his mind."

Rob had expected this reply and sighed deeply.

"Maybe we can describe each one to you. There's no mistaking Smokey. We can write it all down."

"You do that, and if we see what appears to be your herd, I promise to see what we can do," the colonel replied. "If there are soldiers or any person of authority there, I will make an effort to get their cooperation. That is the best I can do."

Although deeply disappointed, both boys thanked the officer and returned to their tent to think. It was late that night before they had a plan — one born of desperation. Before they put it into operation, they would have to wait for the horses from Fort Ellice to arrive. They hoped to get news of their mother and father from the drivers, for, Smokey or no, they would return if they were needed at home.

The horses from Fort Ellice arrived two days later. Both Rob and Luke breathed a sigh of relief when they saw that McKay wasn't one of the men who drove the animals. McKay wouldn't only have scolded them, he would have made sure they returned with him. Instead, Joe Boleau, one of the clerks at the fort, was the man in charge. They knew him only by sight.

Joe Boleau knew them, though. He stood watching them approach, hands on hips, his black eyebrows were beetled in a frown. "Though you are bad boys, I, Boleau, am happy to see you."

Rob's heart sank for a moment, and then he threw back his shoulders and extended his hand. "We're mighty glad to see you, too, Mr. Boleau. I'm hoping you have news of my folks."

Boleau nodded several times very slowly before he replied. "Me, I have news. Good news. Your papa and mama are well, though the wound heals slowly."

"Whew!" Rob said. "That's a relief to hear."

"Is Dad getting in the hay?" Luke asked.

"Factor McKay took three men up to help, else he would have been here with the horses."

"Even better," Rob said.

The long silence that followed was broken when Rob extended his hand again, "Thanks, Mr. Boleau. We're obliged to you."

Boleau shook hands with both Rob and Luke, staring at them sternly, then said. "We leave with Inspector Jarvis and his wagons in a few days."

Rob felt his face grow warm — he hated lying. "Sure, Mr. Boleau," he said lamely. Luke merely nodded, and they turned away to walk back to their tent.

"We still going with the same plan?" Luke asked.

"Of course," Rob replied.

* * *

During the five days of rest that followed, Colonel French had been planning the division of his troops. For two days the large group of sick men had been carefully placed into wagons under Inspector Jarvis' watchful eyes. Sergeant-Major Sam Steele was everywhere, helping tie more than fifty worn out horses behind the wagons and herding the weakest of cows and calves into the circle of the dozens of wagons and carts that were his responsibility.

Rob and Luke sat on their mounts and watched the hive of activity, hoping that they would have a chance to talk to Denny. Their plan's success depended on his cooperation. After an hour had passed, he drew his animal to a halt beside them.

"Wonder where we're supposed to ride," Luke said gloomily. "Probably with the cows."

Denny shook his head sympathetically, and when he spoke, Rob was happy to see another side of the joking and laughing man. "I know how you feel, lads, and I'm sorry as can be. It's painful to dream of making your family proud only to have your hardest efforts fail."

Rob allowed his shoulders to slump. "It wasn't just to make our dad proud. He's been working more'n fifteen years building our farm and getting breeding stock. He sold one or two now and then, but this time he was going to sell about a dozen. This time we were going to get some things we been doing without."

Denny shook his head. "What kind of things?"

Rob felt a little embarrassed now, and didn't answer. Dad wouldn't want him whining and making it sound like they had a hard life.

"Come on, lad," Denny said gently. "What is it you wanted?"

Rob wished he hadn't said anything. It was one thing to try to get Denny's sympathy and another to lay bare the affairs of his family; but he didn't want to be rude. "Well, Mum was hoping to have her organ shipped to her. She likes music a lot. And Dad was planning to get one of those machines for cutting hay that horses pull."

"And what about you?" Denny asked.

"I was hoping for a saddle."

Denny turned to Luke. "And you? What do you want?"

Luke shrugged. "Nothing."

"Dad works hard," Rob said, "and so does Mum. And in one night those wolfers took it all away."

Denny reached over to touch Rob's shoulder. "He can begin again, Rob. And now he has you and Luke to help."

"I don't know that he can start again. We won't have enough money to buy a stud horse and maybe not even enough to buy oats if we did."

Luke sounded desperate. "If we could just get to Fort Benton," he said, "I know we could get our herd back."

"You know your herd is in Fort Benton?" Denny asked, his face wore a look of surprise. "How could you be sure of that?"

Reminding himself to keep a sad, defeated look pasted on his face, Rob said, "The new guide — Morrow's his name. He helped the wolfers drive our herd down to the border, and he thinks they're going to Fort Benton."

"We're so close, and Colonel French says we can't go down when he does and get our horses," Luke chimed in. "We have to go back home with Inspector Jarvis."

"Just a moment," Denny appeared perplexed. "You say Colonel French is going south to Fort Benton? How do you know this?"

Letting his unhappy mask drop, Rob responded eagerly. "We heard him say as much when he was talking to the new guide."

"I seemed to have missed quite a bit," Denny said. "I wasn't aware that we had a new guide much less that the colonel is going to Fort Benton. Perhaps you could tell me when this big event is to take place?"

"We don't know," Rob replied.

"Just wish we were going, too," Luke said glumly. Rob shot a quick scowl at his brother — a warning not to overdo it.

Rob held his breath as he watched Denny rub his

clean shaven chin thoughtfully. "Let me think about this, lads. There must be something that can be done."

After Denny rode over to where the wagons were being loaded for the trek to Fort Ellice, Luke's face split with a wide grin. "We did it! He's on our side."

Rob was elated, too. They never would have thought of this if McDuff hadn't filled them in on Denny's background. From him, they had learned that Inspector Denny was the younger son in a wealthy family in Ireland, where the tradition was to leave the family estate to the older son and give the younger one money to start a life somewhere else. Inspector Denny had chosen to cross the Atlantic and set up a large cattle farm somewhere in Midwestern United States. McDuff said his intent was to prove his worth to his autocratic father. Denny's luck had been bad, however, and he struggled against drought and a bad market for four years before losing all his money and being forced to give up his land.

"And if anybody can think of a way for us to get to Fort Benton," Rob said, "he can."

CHAPTER TEN

Almost two weeks after Inspector Jarvis and his collection of sick men and animals left for Fort Ellice, the boys learned that they had only partly succeeded in their plan to ride down to Fort Benton with Colonel French. The first step was to write a short letter to their parents explaining what they were planning to do. Denny then slipped the letter into the small packet of mail Colonel French was having delivered to the chief factor at Fort Ellice. Rob and Luke knew McKay would send it on to the McCann farm.

To confirm the story that they were parting from the troops, they revealed the name of the plant that helped repel mosquitoes and even found a patch to show Dr. Kittson. Later they made their farewells to the men of F Troop and left the camp, following behind the plodding cattle that Inspector Jarvis was taking to Fort Ellice.

The entire camp was on parade, saluting the troops as they left. Following Denny's advice, Luke and Rob waited until the slow moving caravan had travelled about ten miles before they rode up to one of the troopers stationed at the end of the line and informed him that they had changed their minds and were going back to the main train. The trooper — one they had never met — was clearly confused. Rob figured he had no idea who they were and probably didn't care; but at least he would be able to explain to Inspector Jarvis in case they were missed, else there would have been a search.

Hidden by the trees lining the Souris River, they approached the busy camp with caution. If anyone in F Troop was surprised to see them, he didn't say a word, but when Bagley discovered they had returned he was delighted. Both Rob and Luke immediately joined the men, who were hauling coal to the forge just outside the camp where the blacksmith was hammering out horseshoes. Nearly everyone in D Troop had been ordered to hunt for game, and they succeeded in bagging a dozen deer. The carcasses were skinned and cooked, along with a plentiful supply of ducks and geese, and enough meat was packed away to last a week. The horses were also greatly improved by the rest and good grass for grazing, so the train set off once again the following day.

When it was safe to do so, Rob and Luke rode openly with the F Troop urging the straggling cattle and extra horses forward. Because so many of the weaker animals had been sent to Fort Ellice, it was easy, at first, for F Troop to keep up and camp at night with the rest of the train. That was true until a few days away from Roche Percée when Rob realized that they had turned north, away from the boundary line; the stony trail they followed was marked only by the tracks of the horses and wagons ahead and seemed to be on a gentle, uphill grade. Once again F Troop fell behind and camped alone at night.

Two days later, F Troop caught up with the company, which had been resting after pulling wagons and nine-pound guns to the top of a long, low hill. Rob's heart jerked a little when, as they sat hidden in the back of a wagon, Luke poked him and pointed. They were passing half a dozen horses lying on their sides, barely breathing. Luke whispered, "They won't be pulling guns or anything else anymore."

They both poked their heads from the back of the wagon when it came to a sudden stop. "Some of the men don't look so good either," Rob whispered back to his brother. "See over there."

Shading their eyes, they both looked to where Rob had pointed. A man was sitting doubled over on his horse, both arms crossed tightly across his stomach.

"It's McDuff!" Rob said, and started to jump from the wagon.

"Wheest!" Luke said, grabbing his brother's arm. "Dr. Kittson's there. He'll tend to him."

Rob sat back. There wasn't anything he could do anyway. McDuff was one of the strongest and hardest-working men in the troop, and for him to fall like that meant it was probably more serious than stomach upset from the water or spoiled meat. They had all suffered from that, more than once.

After McDuff was helped into a wagon and his horse led away, the line of red coats began to move again. As soon as the other four troops were a safe distance ahead, Rob and Luke slid out from the moving wagon and ran to find their horses. They rode in search of Inspector Denny and found him at the far back of the line, riding his own animal and leading another. As they cantered closer, both boys spoke at once. "What's the matter with McDuff?"

Denny halted his horse and replied, "Dr. Kittson reported that six others have fever and are feeling cold with cramps in the stomach, too. As you would expect, our McDuff refused to admit he was sick until he could no longer stand." He looked at the pair of troubled faces and added, "Don't you worry, lads. He's been taken up the line, and with Dr. Kittson to look after him he is sure to get better quickly — and so will the others."

Somehow Rob wasn't comforted, and he knew Luke felt the same. In spite of their fear of being discovered, they decided they would see McDuff for themselves as soon as there was an opportunity. However, because all the exhausted or sick horses were put back under F Troop's charge, they had fallen two days behind the main force again. Denny instructed the men who rode to the main camp for food for his troop to inquire about McDuff, and each night they reported back that he was still being cared for by the doctor.

Two days later, F Troop caught up with the main force where they were camped at Old Wives Lake. From there, Colonel French had sent Colonel Macleod with several carts and men south to Wood Mountain, a small village made up of Métis families and the well-supplied men who were marking the boundary. On the day after F Troop joined the camp, the colonel arrived with the oats for the horses they so desperately needed, as well as a large supply of pemmican and dried meat for the troops.

The following day Rob and Luke managed to run, crouched down, to the wagon where McDuff was lying very still. "Mac," Rob whispered. "Mac, you awake?"

There was no answer.

Luke put his hands on the end board and swung up and inside. Rob watched anxiously as his brother felt the man's chest for a heartbeat. A limp hand rose from the blanket and touched Luke on the arm. Rob climbed into the wagon and dropped to his knees beside Luke.

"Are you hurting?" Luke whispered; to Rob he murmured, "He's burning up with fever."

"Nay," McDuff responded in a hoarse whisper. "I'm but having a bit of a nap."

"Dr. Kittson said you're going to be fine, soon as we get good water," Rob fibbed, forgetting that the doctor wouldn't have known that he and Luke were still with the train.

McDuff hadn't forgotten. His arms thrashed weakly as he tried to sit up, and his voice rose above the whisper. "Lads, you're supposed to be hiding from ..." His words trailed off and he began to cough.

Rob and Luke stood by helplessly, wishing they had soothing water to give their friend; but their canteens had emptied days ago and the water in Old Wives Lake was murky with alkali. Some of the men had drunk from it and were complaining already of stomach pains.

Rob stood suddenly, banging his head on the top of the wagon. "I'm going to find some water."

Luke looked up at his brother. "Where?"

"I'll swim out into the lake. Maybe the water's cleaner there."

"Don't you dare," Luke protested. "It's probably all sand out there. Remember what happened to Denny?"

Rob began to slip off his jacket, and McDuff's hands lifted. "No need, Rob," he gasped. "I don't want …" He paused as the wagon began to shake as Denny crawled into the front followed by Colonel Macleod.

With only a stern glance at each of the boys, the colonel moved to McDuff's side and lifted the sick man's head with one hand. In the other he held a tin cup filled with water. "Drink a bit of this, trooper," he said. "It's not from the lake. Just a bit farther up we found a creek, and the water is much better."

With a hoarse "Thank you, Sir," McDuff swallowed a few drops of the water, then lay back and closed his eyes.

Colonel Macleod half-rose, and turned to leave. Over his shoulder he said, "Colonel French intends to see those who are ill, so you two best make yourselves scarce. I'll attend to you later."

"Out you go," the inspector said before they could protest. "I'll stay here until the doctor returns."

Reluctantly, Rob and Luke whispered goodbye and jumped from the back of the wagon. They walked slowly to F Troop, too worried about McDuff to care who might see them. Neither of them spoke until they had almost reached their tent, which was pitched behind the last wagon. Then Luke said, "He sure didn't look like Mac. His face and arms are so thin."

"Mum says fever burns the fat right off you." Rob felt a wave of homesickness wash over him and he wished he had never ridden away from the snug cabin.

It didn't help that Luke said, "I wish Mum was here to tend to Mac. She'd have him back on a horse in no time."

Seeking an outlet for his sadness, Rob snapped back at his brother. "And you'd like her to be here, I guess, with no water that's fit to drink and nothing to eat but half-baked bread and half-rotten meat!"

Luke stared back as though he'd been struck, and immediately Rob apologized. "I know better'n that, Luke. I guess I'm just worried about Mac and about how we can get down to Fort Benton and if we ..." he hesitated. "And if we did the right thing coming here."

Rob nodded. He was beginning to worry about how they were going to get home.

"We did the right thing, Rob," Luke said firmly. "With Dad hurt, it only makes sense. Who else was there to try to find our herd?"

Some of Rob's confidence returned. They would find a way to get to Fort Benton; they had to. And tomorrow morning they would walk bold as can be up to the wagon where Mac lay and ride to the next camp with him.

But morning came too late.

CHAPTER ELEVEN

The next morning, McDuff was laid to rest in a shallow grave under a pyramid of piled rocks. All the men had turned out on the stony plain under a pitiless sun. It was obvious that they had cleaned and brushed their tattered uniforms as best they could, and each troop lined up on parade. Trooper Bagley sat erect on his horse beside the officers, bugle under his arm. Men and mounts were motionless, and even the air was still as Colonel French read the service in a clear, ringing voice. When he recited the words "ashes to ashes and dust to dust," Rob forced back the sob rising in his throat and, instead of listening, tried to concentrate on the mosquito sucking blood from a nearby officer's cheek, wondering if he'd swat it. But the trooper kept rigidly still, and the mosquito, satisfied, drifted away just as Colonel French stopped speaking and Colonel Macleod moved forward to take his place.

"Most of you knew Constable McDuff," Macleod began, "for he was a friend and a comrade to any man who would wish him to be. You heard him playing the tunes of Scotland on his wooden flute around the campfire at night. But he was a private person, and perhaps few of you know his reasons for leaving the land he loved.

"For a number of years he and his young wife had kept a croft on the Isle of Skye, but the weather failed them and they lost their crops for three years running. There was no work to be had, and like many others, Mac came to Canada to work and to save. His hopes and his dreams were to return to Scotland in two years with enough money to purchase another small farm."

The officer paused for a thoughtful moment. "I was too young for memories of Scotland when my family came to this land, but I share his appreciation for the poems of the great Robert Burns. Many a time I heard McDuff read from the wee book he carried. It wasn't always easy to understand the Gaelic words when he spoke them aloud. But there is one I remember that — by changing it just a bit — will serve as farewell to Constable Angus McDuff."

Colonel Macleod paused again, then clasped his hands behind his back and stared up at the sky. "His heart's in the Highlands," he began. "His heart is not here. His heart's in the Highlands a-chasing the deer. Chasing the wild deer and following the roe. His heart's in the Highlands wherever he goes."

The knot in Rob's chest had grown more painful than he could bear. He slipped away then, followed by Luke, back to the F Troop's cluster of wagons. The high, quavering notes of the bugle followed them.

Shortly after the funeral, the train of men moved out, eventually stopping a few miles away at Old Wife's Creek where there was both good water and grass for the horses. Word rapidly spread that Colonel French intended to leave the weakest horses and cattle with a few men and wagons to camp there. They would be picked up by some of the police who, after the mission was accomplished, would return to the East. The spot quickly became known as Cripple Camp.

His duties taken care of, the forever-restless Denny rode up and beckoned for Rob and Luke to follow. "In spite of the magnificent bounty Macleod brought us, I need meat that can be roasted over a campfire."

Although Rob felt heartsore and listless, he looked forward to doing something that might distract from his sense of loss.

They rode south along the creek for more than two miles, seeing nothing but a badger darting into a hole beside a clump of prairie grass, until they came upon a Native camp around a bend. Inspector Denny jerked back on his reins, and motioned the boys to silence. The camp was small, not more than five men and a dozen women and children. They had been eating and rose to stare, first at Denny then at each of the two boys. Denny cleared his throat then raised his hand in greeting. "Good morning," he said. Covering their mouths with their hands, the women and children giggled. The men were silent, their gazes stony.

Rob and Luke looked at each other, wondering if they should interrupt. "We come in peace," Denny said. The women and children giggled again.

It was then Rob noticed the rifles lying near the men's feet, and he decided it would be all right to interrupt. "This is an Assiniboine camp," he said to Denny. "We know a few words."

Clearly relieved, Denny said, "Go ahead. Tell them we come in peace."

"I'll tell them," Luke said, moving his horse beside Denny's. With gestures and a few halting words, he relayed the message; and the Natives appeared to relax. There were more words and hands beckoning before Rob said, "Think they want us to get down and eat with them."

Luke nodded. Denny's response was quick: "No thanks. Tell them that we just ate and are going hunting."

Luke nodded toward the Native men who were still gesturing for them to dismount. "It's not too good to turn down an invitation. Indians think that's kind of an insult."

"Oh, well." Denny sighed as he dismounted. "When in Rome...."

The three of them sat cross-legged like their hosts, and helped themselves to pemmican by digging into the large clay pot with their hands. The pemmican was surprisingly good. It had been mixed with berries, and if it contained tiny stones or weeds, Rob didn't find any. He ate sparingly, though. These people didn't look as well fed as the Assiniboine back home. They made conversation with some difficulty, but Rob and Luke managed to learn that this camp was part of a larger one heading for prairie land about six days away to hunt buffalo. Denny had been admiring two of the horses foraging nearby, and suggested the boys ask if they were for sale. Their question elicited the emphatic shaking of heads. When the group's elder spoke next, Rob and Luke leaped to their feet.

Rob's heart was racing as he turned to a startled Inspector Denny. "They said they met some men with plenty of horses to sell." His throat was suddenly dry, but he managed to ask the elder to describe the horses. After a lengthy conversation among themselves, one of the Natives told him that most were grey as the earth, but the stallion's mane and tail were as pale as the moon.

Almost before the man finished speaking, Rob began to ask where they saw the herd and which way was it going. The man shrugged, and the group began to shift uneasily on their feet. "Easy, Rob," cautioned Luke. "They can tell we're excited and are probably wondering if we're going to blame them for something."

Denny had risen and had been waiting patiently, looking from the men in the camp back to Rob and Luke. "Would someone please tell me what has you two so upset?"

"It's our herd," Rob said. "They saw them south of here." He turned away to speak to the elder. This time he fastened a friendly smile on his face and used a lighter tone. The Assiniboines relaxed again and had another short conference between themselves before they answered. This time Rob thanked them with some vaguely remembered words in their language. Forcing himself to be calm, he said, "It was about two weeks ago. They think they were heading west toward the high hills."

"Just what we need — more hills to pull those blasted guns and injure more horses!" Denny muttered.

He, too, seemed careful not let his face betray his feelings.

"If Colonel French had kept us close to the boundary line, we might've crossed their trail," Luke said angrily. "Then he could have had some good horses. Why'd he turn north? Are we close to Fort Whoop-Up?"

"Perhaps we should talk about this later," Denny replied. He moved closer to the Assiniboines and in a long, flowery speech thanked them for their hospitality. "Translate that. There's a good lad," he said to Luke and mounted his horse.

As they rode away, Denny said, "We all know that I'm not one of the favoured few under Colonel French's command. I only become aware of his plans thanks to Colonel Macleod."

"Right," Rob said, trying not to show his impatience. "Where are we going then?"

"If I knew that," Denny began cheerfully. "I would know more than our glorious leader. Apparently his distrust of our latest guide has grown from faint to serious, and he's relying more and more on the Palliser map and prismatic compass he carries."

"We saw one of those at Fort Ellice," Luke said. "Some men of the Hudson's Bay Company came upriver in big canoes, and one of the fancy dressed ones had one of those things. Remember Rob? Everybody wanted to see it work, but we went outside so they wouldn't see us laughing at their fancy outfits."

Luke didn't usually speak so long, but Rob figured it was because he, too, was excited that the Natives had seen the herd.

They were nearing the camp now. Denny pulled his mount to a halt and looked at his companions thoughtfully. "It occurs to me," he said "that there may be some thought of leaving you here to be picked up later with the rest."

"Oh, no!" Luke protested.

At the exact same moment, Rob said, "We won't stay.

"Does Colonel French know we're still here?" Rob asked. He had been hoping Colonel Macleod had been so busy getting supplies for the troops that he'd forgotten about them. During the funeral service, they had been careful to keep hidden behind the troopers. Other than that, they'd managed to keep back with F Troop. Rob wondered now if any of the men in Denny's troop knew that he and Luke weren't supposed to be there. He wasn't particularly worried, though: all the men were their friends.

Denny was replying to his question. "Far as I am aware he doesn't, else I would have been the first to receive the full force of his wrath."

"Are you and Colonel French enemies?" Luke asked,

and Denny laughed aloud.

"No, Luke, not at all. That is but a joke around the campfires. Unfortunately, I have had several mishaps that came to his attention."

Rob was curious now. "What kind of mishaps? Do you mean like riding your horse into the alkali bed?"

Denny shook his head and smiled ruefully. "Colonel Macleod kindly didn't report that unfortunate accident, but it does appear as though I have a talent for displeasing our Commissioner French."

Rob persisted. "How?"

Denny's eyes twinkled, but he didn't reply. Instead he turned his horse, calling over his shoulder. "I best report that Indians are camped nearby. The colonel may wish to take our guides over to question them."

"What about our herd?" Rob asked. "Maybe you could mention that the Assiniboines saw them. If you were to catch those horse thieves, we'd sell some of the herd to him."

Back in their tent, Luke and Rob daydreamed aloud about what would happen if they caught up with the thieves. They were certain that they would step up and claim the herd if the men tried to sell the horses to Colonel French. "Just think of it, Luke," Rob said. "Mum would laugh and cry at the same time, just because we're back safe, and …"

"And Dad would be laughing, too, and not mad at us for being away so long when we show him all the money we'll get for the horses."

They stopped talking, and the glow in their eyes faded. What if they returned with neither horses nor money?

CHAPTER TWELVE

The boys waited under the twisted limbs of an old cottonwood tree near their tent. "Denny's sure taking his time," Rob grumbled. A long bank of fleecy clouds was beginning to turn gold, reflecting the setting sun, and still the inspector hadn't returned.

At first, after hearing that a herd of horses had been sighted by the Assiniboine, they had been happy and excited, certain that their search was nearing its end. Luke figured that since nearly half of the horses the police had started with had died or been left behind by now, Colonel French was sure to see the good sense of trying to find the strong prairie horses the wolfers had stolen. Rob and Luke had even discussed their asking price. As the day wore on, however, their joy dimmed and certainty was replaced by serious thought.

"Denny said they've been on the march for about seven hundred miles now and still have a ways to go," Rob said. "If they don't find ours, by the time they get where they're going they'll be out of horses."

Luke nodded. "We should remind Colonel French about the time our horses pulled up the wagon when the oxen couldn't. He's sure to want the herd."

"But not Smokey," Rob reminded his brother.

Luke started to reply, but was interrupted when Inspector Denny appeared from behind the tree. Both boys scrambled to their feet. "What'd he say?" they asked in unison.

"I had no opportunity to mention your stolen horses," Denny replied. "The colonel was a mile or two away having a powwow with a small band of Sioux."

Rob felt a chill up his spine as Luke muttered, "Jings!"

"We're doubling the guard," Denny said. "I need you two to take a turn now so I have enough men for later."

Rob tried to keep the quaver out of his voice, "What're they doing here? You think it's because they're angry that the police are here?"

Denny shrugged. "That's doubtful. They don't appear to be hostile and there are women and children with them. The Métis drivers say this prairie is a hunting ground for Indians of many tribes — Blackfoot, Gros Ventre, Sioux, Assiniboine, and the Métis, as well."

"What about the little camp of Assiniboine we saw a while ago?" Luke asked. "It'll sure be bad if the Sioux find them."

"I've taken care of that," Denny said, sounding rather pleased with himself. "I dispatched two of our Métis drivers to their camp to warn them, but they had already packed up and left."

Rob figured that was probably a good thing. He'd heard Colonel Macleod remind the men more than once that one of their most important tasks was keeping the peace in this land. Rob wished them luck: ever since he could remember he'd heard tales of raids and big battles between the tribes. Dad had guessed that Luke and his mother were captured during a raid and she was trying to get back to her own people. The big question was: who were her people?

Denny turned to go. "We're doubling the horse guard tonight, so off you go. And bear in mind that it's important that the horses be kept quiet, lest they run off and lose the last of their strength. No shooting at shadows."

Some of the healthier horses were picketed, but most of the thinner ones were hobbled so they could pick at the sparse grass during the night. Few did. Most of them were lying on their sides, their eyes closed. Along with a dozen of the troopers, Rob and Luke each chose a place to watch the hundred or so tired animals. The night was still, the only sounds coming from the murmurs of men sitting around campfires more than a hundred yards away. Time passed with the speed of a snail.

Rob fought sleep by moving slowly back and forth, a few steps to the right and a few steps to the left. His rifle began to slip from his grasp, and his steps faltered. He shook himself again and again, and plodded on. Suddenly he was snapped alert, and a tiny shock darted up his spine. Peering into growing darkness, he could see nothing that would cause alarm. And there were no sounds other than the gentle breathing of a nearby horse. But something wasn't right.

Sharply alert now, Rob tried to make out the outline of his brother. He had been only a dozen or so yards away. Rob's heart skipped a beat; Luke sure wasn't there now. He was reluctant to leave the place he had been assigned to watch the horses, but Luke was more important. Rob moved cautiously through the dry leaves covering the ground. For a moment his heart stopped when he spotted his brother stretched out on the ground, but then he smiled. Poor Luke, he just couldn't stay awake. Rob moved closer and leaned down to tug on Luke's ear. His smile disappeared when he looked at his hand more closely: it was sticky with blood.

He started to shout, but thought better of it. His mind was racing. *All Hell will break loose if I yell. And I gotta take care of Luke.* Rob dropped to his knees to feel for a heartbeat — a move that may have saved his own life, for at that moment a club swooped down, barely missing his head. Rob whirled around and instinctively lashed out, catching a pair of knees that buckled from the blow. A body fell beside him. With lightning swiftness Rob was astride the body pinning it to the ground. In the shadowy light of the slowly rising moon, a young Native boy stared up at him. His eyes showed no fear.

Warily, Rob looked around in the darkness. *What if there are more of them out there? And what do I do with this one?* Beside him, Luke stirred. Rob nudged him with his foot. "Luke," he whispered. "Luke, you all right?"

Luke struggled to a sitting position and rubbed his head. "All right," he mumbled.

Still whispering, Rob spoke more forcefully. "You gotta help me, Luke. I can't sit on this thief for much longer. 'Sides that, he's probably got friends. Go tell Constable Clint."

More awake now, Luke stood and staggered away. Rob looked down again at the slight figure of his captive. He could see that he had no weapon other than the small club lying nearby. His eyes still held no fear, but rather an acceptance of his hopeless situation and, like a blow to his belly, Rob remembered when he had been at the mercy of the three Natives earlier in the journey.

He had managed to appear unafraid, but inside had been scared witless. He hesitated for a long moment, then rolled off the boy and stood. His gesture told his captive to stand. But how to tell him to run? He tried to shoo him away as his mum did with her chickens, but the boy only stared at him suspiciously. Rob wanted him to leave before Luke returned with the constable. Desperately he reached out and clasped the boy's hand and at the same time grasped his shoulder as he had seen the Assiniboines do when they bade farewell to his father. Then he pushed the boy away and waved.

The bewildered boy took a few steps away and looked over his shoulder. Rob waved again, and the boy leaped into the trees. A moment later he reappeared and waved back at Rob before he melted into the night.

"He got away," Rob said when Luke reappeared with the man in charge of the watch. "He won't be back."

The constable nodded. "Likely just some young buck trying to take a horse back to his camp for bragging rights." He peered at Luke, and added, "You did well not to cause a ruckus, Rob. See that your brother gets to the doc and then wake Constable Craig. It's time we're relieved."

The hours before dawn were long, but Rob didn't sleep. He had woken Constable Craig, but much as he argued,

Luke still refused to see the doctor. It wasn't going to be his fault if Colonel French discovered that they were still with the troops. In despair, Rob sat watching his brother sleep, thinking how defenceless he looked. From time to time Rob wiped away the trickle of blood oozing from a growing lump just above Luke's ear. *If he dies of a cracked head, it'll be my fault. If he dies, I'll never go home. It'll be lonely enough if Luke finds his true folks and leaves, but least I might see him from time to time. If he dies....*

Dawn had just begun to send fingers of light through the leaves hanging over the tent when Rob fell over on his side, and slept.

CHAPTER THIRTEEN

Word of the attempted horse robbery had spread through F Troop, and both Rob and Luke were treated like heroes. To ease the headache that had turned Luke's lips white with pain, Denny managed to secure some laudanum from Dr. Kittson by pretending to have a severe headache himself. The trooper who was also F Troop's cook had made pemmican soup with wild onions he had found, and fully baked the bread to tempt Luke to eat. Rob carefully washed the three inch split in Luke's skull and watched anxiously for any sign of infection. In the two days that followed, the lump gradually grew smaller and Luke refused more laudanum. Orders were given: the troopers were to pack up and be ready to move again.

Colonel Macleod and a few constables had gone south twice to buy oats and hay from the well-supplied men who were marking the boundary, and once he'd been able to purchase a dozen horses — all of them dark brown. As the train moved northwest, they sometimes spotted small herds of buffalo, but they were too far in the distance to give chase. They used the pancake-sized dried buffalo dung they found along the way, which burned well in their campfires. Rob figured buffalo were a mixed blessing since they could make good eating, but they chewed off all the grass in their path and turned small creeks to mud.

Some of the men began to grumble over the following days since leaving the fairly comfortable camp at Old Wife's Creek — especially after they set up camp one night in the driving rain and had to ride in sodden clothing while buffeted by a cold wind the next day. A rumour floated through the camp that they were lost, that Colonel French had no idea which way to go. They doubted the very notion that they would ever see the mountains they had heard so much about. Some even began to doubt the existence of the mountains.

On August 25 the advance scouts spotted the Cypress Hills. They also rode into camp that night with two antelope and three deer — a welcome change from pemmican. Rob and Luke weren't impressed, though, and had been silently fuming ever since they left Cripple Camp and turned northwest, when they should have been going southwest. Rob was impatient to get to Fort Benton and perhaps find news of their missing herd. That night, when Inspector Denny joined F Troop for the evening meal, Rob forgot himself and demanded an explanation.

"Seems to me Colonel French must be dumb as a stump if he can't see that he has to go south if he's going to Fort Benton!" As soon as these words left his tongue, Rob regretted them. He knew he had gone too far.

There was dead silence while Denny stared at Rob. But the officer relaxed and reached for the tin teapot. Filling his cup, he said gently, "I know how you feel, Rob, but you must bear this in mind: the purpose of this journey is to bring law and order to this great land. The first step is to catch and stop those ruffians selling whiskey to the Natives. Anything else is second to that."

Rob picked up the stick at his feet and jabbed at the fire with it. He knew he should apologize, but he just couldn't. Luke had almost been killed; they hadn't had a decent meal since they left home, and they were dog-tired. Worst of all, it was starting to look like it was all for nothing.

Denny was still speaking. "We all know where we have been, but it's the colonel who knows how to find the whiskey fort." He paused and looked around at each of the seven men around the campfire. "And that fort is about two or three days from here, with good feed for the horses and shelter for all."

The men were excitedly talking at once. "When do we start?" asked a trooper with an Irish accent. "It's lookin' for a fight with them bad men, I am!"

Denny grinned. "Sit yourself down, McGee. The colonel wants us to rest here for a few days to get men and horses in shape for that fight."

Even the officers expressed both astonishment and unrestrained jubilation when, two days later, Morrow came galloping back from the advance guard and slid to a stop beside the colonel. Word spread quickly down the line: they had reached the meeting of the Bow and Belly Rivers, and the whiskey fort would be nearby.

Denny's F Troop had been lagging behind, as usual. But when they heard the shouts through the still air Denny galloped forward, leaving a cloud of dust behind him. He returned quickly to repeat the guide's announcement.

A mix of feelings whirled through Rob. He had become increasingly worried about Luke, who had grown more and more silent. *Sleeping on a warm bed in the fort, with better food might put some more meat on his skinny frame. But if this is to be the end of our journey, is there any hope of finding the horses? And — empty handed or not — how will we get home? One thing's for sure: it's*

*too late for Colonel French to send us back now, so I can
take Luke up to see Dr. Kittson.*

But the elation was short lived and Rob's worries
had to be put aside when Denny returned from con-
ferring once more with the head of the line. Raising
his voice above the creaking wagons and carts, he said,
"Morrow's made a mistake. This supposed meeting of
two rivers is but a sharp turn in the Saskatchewan River."

There was a chorus of groans, and Denny raised his
voice. "Not all is lost. The Saskatchewan River does lead
to the Bow very soon. That is Colonel French's promise."

There had been a cold drizzle for most of the day,
and when they camped that night it turned into an even
colder downpour. Anxious to keep Luke warm, Rob
briefly considered putting their tent near the fire, but
decided the space around the fire was already crowded
with tents. If he could find a place by one of the wagons that would shelter their tent from the wind, they
might still stay warm and dry. Rob was relieved when
he found the ideal spot — a wagon stopped near a small
outcropping from a low hill. He ran back to the cart
carrying their belongings and hauled out the tent. They
quickly set the tent up beneath the outcropping, and
Rob pushed his brother inside. "I'll see to the horses,"
he said ducking outside where he bumped into Pierre,
one of the wagon drivers.

"Your pardon, mes ami," boomed the Métis. "I should knock, perhaps?"

Rob grinned and bowed low. "Entre, Monsieur."

"Me, I come with the invitation to spend this lovely night in ma maison. It is small, yes? Not to fear. I will move out my furniture, and there is room for all."

Rob didn't hesitate. "Thanks, Pierre, that would be great. Our tent doesn't have a floor, and the ground's already wet."

Silently Luke climbed into the back of the wagon, and Rob tossed their blankets in after him. Pierre handed down the water barrels he carried, and Rob rolled them under the wagon. Then he went to see about their horses.

Sam and Chris were standing were they'd left them, about four yards away. Water bounced off their hanging heads and dripped from their necks. Rob stripped off their saddles, and ran his hand over Sam's sides feeling her ribs through her cold skin. She shivered. He rested his head against her neck for a moment. "Jings, Sam," he whispered, "if Dad saw you like this, he'd have my ears for breakfast." He had a crazy thought then. *Why not try? If Pierre doesn't see me, no one will know.*

Rob gathered the reins dangling from both horses and led them to the tent beside the wagon. He quickly collapsed the tent, and reached for Sam's bridle. At first, she refused to back under the shelf of rock, but with

Rob's tugs on the reins and whispered encouragement; she finally moved under it and stood next to the wagon. Chris, on the other hand, seemed to feel any shelter was better than none and needed no urging at all. Carefully, Rob draped the flattened tent over their backs. "There now," he whispered, "it's close quarters for sure, but you can keep each other warm. I'll be back with your oats. Best you eat slow. It's the last we got."

Through the cold, wet night, Sam and Chris stood side-by-side, and emerged, albeit stiffly, in the morning; but five other horses weren't as fortunate, and had died over night. Rob started wishing that he'd wake up from this nightmare.

Two days later Denny's promise, that they were near the end of their journey, seemed to be fulfilled. When F Troop caught up with the rest of the train they could see wagons and carts had stopped in shallow swale, and beyond them men and horses were lined up. Denny and his men rode up the low hill to join them; Rob and Luke followed.

Far below, the wide, shining river snaked along between high bluffs as far as the eye could see. Rob turned to his brother. "Look at that, Luke. Must be that's the Saskatchewan River, and someplace around it there's supposed to be the two rivers that feed into it, and that's where we find the whiskey traders."

Luke smiled weakly. "Maybe the ones that have our horses!"

"Right." Rob stared down the hill. "But how the heck do we get down there?"

Colonel Macleod rode over to confer with Denny and the men of F Troop. "We camp here tonight, and tomorrow we will follow the river west to the junction of the Bow and Belly Rivers. However, we must first find a way to get ourselves down to the rivers." Looking down the line of men, his let his eyes rest upon Rob and Luke. Without a smile, he continued, "That would be a good task for our stowaways. Ride west no more than twenty miles and find us a path."

Without a word, Rob and Luke turned their horses. "You okay, Luke? Maybe you should sit here and wait until I get back."

"Don't be daft," Luke replied curtly and rode on, both of them at a steady lope.

About four hours had passed when they heard a rumble like distant thunder. Instinctively they looked up expecting to see thunderheads but only wispy trails of white drifted through the bright blue sky. Puzzled, Rob turned in his saddle, his eyes searching the empty plain. Suddenly Luke shouted, "Jings! Rob look!" He was pointing ahead to a black line surging toward them in the distance. Buffalo!

They were coming faster than a shot from a rifle. Rob felt himself go weak. "We gotta get out of here."

Their only chance was to try to outrun them. With a quick jerk on her reins and a kick in her ribs, Sam leaped around and began to race back along the ridge above the river. Rob glanced over his shoulder to make sure Luke was close behind. As they flew over the hard ground, Rob imagined the hoof beats were closer. For one scary moment he pictured the mass of running beasts pouring over them like a dark and deadly wave.

After several seconds, which felt like minutes, he realized he was wrong. The noise was different somehow. Cautiously, Rob turned his head, and saw that Luke was also looking back as he rode. They pulled their horses to a halt. The buffalo were no longer heading their way but were pouring over the side of the bluff, heading down to the river.

"Whew!" Rob exclaimed through lips so dry they stuck together. "That was close!"

They stood in silence, watching the amazing spectacle. Thousands of buffalo were swimming across the river below, and several thousand more were flowing down the hill leaving a cloud of dust in their wake. When the last of the animals made it down to the river,

Rob and Luke rode more than a mile to the hundred-foot-wide gap where the huge beasts had plunged down the hill. It was plain that the path had been used before: the soil was worn down to bare rock in some places and hard packed in the rest. It sloped gradually to the river where the buffalo were swimming across, the sun gleaming brightly on the mass of wet backs.

"Jings!" Rob said shakily. "Good thing we didn't get this far else we might have been riding down there around the same time those buffalo started running down."

It was then that Luke spoke thoughtfully as he stared down at the astonishing scene. "I think I've seen this before — saw buffalo swimming the river."

Rob glanced at his brother quickly. With a stab of fear, he wondered if Luke was remembering more. Was it from here that he and his mum were taken?

CHAPTER FOURTEEN

Rob and Luke rested their tired horses before heading back to the camp. It was nearly dusk when they saw that Colonel Macleod and two constables had ridden out to look for them. Although the colonel didn't say anything about their tardy arrival, Rob sensed he was relieved to see them; when Rob reported that, about fifteen miles from the camp, they had found a way down to the river, all he said was "Well done," and turned his horse to ride back to the camp.

Luke was silent and thoughtful on their return to F Troop. And that night, before bedding down, Rob blurted out, "Could be one of the stories we read about the West that's making you think you saw big herds of buffalo before. Maybe you dreamed about them."

Luke gave his brother a startled look, and shrugged

his shoulders. "I don't know, might be. I been trying to remember. Seems like I was sitting in front of somebody on a horse watching them run."

Rob couldn't think of a sensible argument to stop Luke from thinking about his Native folks. Frustrated, he lay back on the hard boards of the wagon, and pulled his blankets up to his ears.

The sun wasn't yet up when the harsh shouts of "Up and at 'em!" filled the air. Groaning, Pierre called from the other end of the wagon, "I must go back to sleep. My wife was about to serve me breakfast."

Rob felt a thrill of excitement. This might be the day they'd actually find their missing herd. He threw off his blankets and pulled on his tattered boots. Beside him, Luke rose more slowly. As though reading Rob's thoughts, he said, "I'm almost afraid to find the fort. If the wolfers aren't there, we got no where else to look."

Rob refused to be afraid. "Not so, Luke. There's still Fort Benton. We could get there somehow." He kept his own nagging worry to himself: what if the horses had been sold to the boundary markers that came from the West or those from the South? They would never find them then.

The troops had long since run out of flour and salt for bread, but it was quick work to roast a few strips of buffalo meat over the fire. Within an hour of the wake-up call, the line of men was on the march — still an imposing sight, even if few of the red coats had survived the journey. Instead many of the tattered red jackets with their shiny buttons had been traded to passing Natives for buckskin shirts and warm moccasins that came up to the knee.

It took longer for the wagons and carts to get down to the river bottom than it had the buffalo, but the men worked hard and eagerly to keep them from rolling too fast. They were all excited about the possibility of reaching their journey's end. Colonel French had watched their efforts and, when all horses, men, and wagons were on level ground, he gave the signal to start west.

They had travelled only a few miles when word passed down the line that A Troop had reached the confluence of the Bow and Belly River. Rob felt an electric thrill run up his spine. Fort Whoop-Up! He slapped Sam's rear and rode forward, Luke close behind.

When they passed the lead wagons and reached the mounted men, the two boys slowed their horses. Something was wrong. Instead of preparing for action, horses and men were standing still and a low murmur was drifting down the line. Rob slowly urged Sam forward a few paces, followed by Luke, before pausing to stare. He was stunned with shock. Ahead were three sagging, roofless cabins. As his eyes travelled back to the double line of men, they found Colonel French mounted beside

Colonel Macleod. His head was no longer high, and his shoulders slumped as he stared at what he had thought would be the end of the long pursuit.

When Colonel French turned his horse to face his men they immediately grew silent. He cleared his throat and, straightening his shoulders, announced in firm voice, "It would seem that our information has been incorrect, and we have not reached our goal. Clearly these cabins are not Fort Whoop-Up. In addition, the land around the meeting of these two rivers is no better than the rough prairie we have ridden over these past days. In spite of these handicaps, we will not falter. We will carry on until our mission is accomplished."

The entire force continued to move beside the deep and rushing Belly River for more than a dozen miles before they found a place to cross. New orders were given: Inspector Walsh was to take seventy men and horses up to Fort Edmonton; Inspector Walker and a few of his men were to follow the Belly River looking for any signs of another fort; and Inspector Denny and his men were to go up the Bow River. Rob and Luke joined that group without waiting to be asked.

The country around the Bow was some of the poorest they had come across on the whole trip. The soil was either sandy or clay, studded with rocks of all sizes, and covered with small hills and dips in the trail they made. Rob figured they had ridden about twenty miles without a sign of life except for a pair of hawks soaring overhead. He wondered how the four Métis, who had come with them, could laugh as they rode, even singing occasionally. His own mouth and throat were parched, and he wished Denny would stop more often so they could go down to the Bow River and drink the clear, rushing water.

One of the Métis guides shot a buffalo during the morning ride and, once they set up camp, found enough bushes to make a fire. They cooked the best pieces by impaling the chunks of meat on thick sticks held over the fire. Rob's mouth was watering so badly from the delicious smell of cooking meat that he could barely wait for it to be done enough to eat. When he finished chewing the tough but tasty strips he waited for Levaillee to wrap up yet another of his endless jokes to ask, "Where did the colonel's information come from? I mean," he waved his arm to encompass the land around them, "about this land being so fertile and grassy?"

When no one replied, Levaillee spoke up. "These rivers come from the mountains. I think those who have seen the land at the headwaters found much to admire. They must have believed that it was the same everywhere by the river and said so without looking at the land farther afield."

"Some of the men don't believe there are any mountains to see," Luke said.

Levaillee laughed and pointed west. "Oh, the mountains are there to see. I haven't looked at them myself, but I have heard much of them."

It was cold in the tent, colder than usual, and Rob slept fitfully. During the night he slipped his second blanket over Luke, who was beginning to cough. Morning was no better, but when the sun rose it melted the mist hanging over the river and revealed a small band of antelope drinking on the other side. They spotted the men and, in an instant, they were gone.

The group agreed to forgo breakfast and be on their way, hoping that they would find something for their mounts to graze on not far ahead. It was late afternoon when they turned their horses up on a low ridge above the river so that they could see into the distance. To their surprise, they spotted two men running on foot. Denny urged his horse into a run and the rest of his companions followed, but the pair leaped down into a ravine before they could stop them.

"Stay here," Denny ordered Rob and Luke, and beckoned to the Métis guides to follow him. Rob gasped when he saw about five dozen Native men pop out of the ravine, their guns pointing at Denny and the Métis.

Denny stopped, raised one hand, and held it forward in a gesture of friendship, but the men didn't respond. Rob couldn't hear what the Métis called out to them, which didn't seem to help anyhow; the Natives dropped back into the ravine far enough so that only their heads and the muzzles of the guns could be seen.

Rob wasn't surprised that they didn't fire the guns: he figured that they were muzzle loaders so their bullets wouldn't fly more than fifty feet, far short of where Denny and the Métis were standing their horses. Finally, one the Natives waved what appeared to be a scalp, inspiring Denny's companions to ride away; after a moment, he followed. When Rob and Luke joined them they looked a bit shamefaced, and Levaillee was trying to explain to Denny. "I think they are Sioux war party. I think they're waiting for others to come. We must leave."

Denny sighed deeply. "If they are Sioux, why didn't they try to attack us? We were outnumbered."

"It is my belief that they have lost their horses and wait for more to be brought."

Denny considered it and shrugged. "Very well. We will continue up the river for a few more miles nevertheless before we head back to camp."

Levaillee and his friends did not seem happy about this, but they followed Denny as he rode eastward, making a wide circle around the ravine. Over the next few days, they travelled upriver almost thirty more miles — always at night, in case the Sioux were following, but they didn't see them again. When they turned back, though, they saw tracks following them for several miles. When they arrived at the main camp, Inspector Denny reported the incident to Colonel French and learned that they had indeed encountered a war party, but it was Assiniboine.

"Sorry, lads," Denny said later when he joined his troop around the campfire. "Had I known they were Assiniboine, I would have had you speak to them."

Rob chuckled. Assiniboine, or not, he didn't fancy having a chat with a war party. "Wonder what happened to their horses."

"Apparently," Denny replied, "while we were away a group of white traders stopped here. They told the colonel that they had been attacked and robbed by the Assiniboine warriors. All their horses were taken, as well as wagon loads of goods they were taking to trade with the Blackfoot. When the Blackfoot warriors heard about the attack, a large war party went after the Assinboines and took the goods and every horse they had."

Rob grinned. "I'm feeling a fondness for these Blackfoot warriors. If things had worked out different, those Assiniboines might've had more scalps!"

"We'll be moving again, lads," Denny said, "as soon as Walsh and his men return. I persuaded the colonel that they couldn't make it to Fort Edmonton. You saw for yourselves how bare the prairie land is to the North. He won't find even a little blade of grass for the horses to fight over."

The usually silent Constable Clint, who had been stirring the campfire, threw away his stick and said crossly, "It's not like we have much more right here. Winter's coming on without a sign of feed or shelter for the horses."

Or the men, Rob thought.

Denny cocked one eyebrow and grinned at the constable. "Mr. Clint, have you so little faith in our glorious leader? I said we are moving again — this time some eighty miles south. You can see the hills from here — the Sweet Grass Hills."

Earlier, one of the men had pointed out that the hills were almost on the boundary line. Rob and Luke looked at each other, confusion showing on their faces. It was Pierre who asked the question they were all thinking: "And why is that, M'sieu? Is this where Fort Whoop-Up is now believed to be?"

Denny shook his head. "No, I think the colonel is starting to doubt that there is a Fort Whoop-Up at all. He has a plan to cross the boundary line and ride down to Fort Benton for supplies and to send messages by telegraph to his superiors in Ottawa."

Rob looked at his brother and knew that Luke was as excited as he was. His mind was working overtime: depending on who went with the colonel, maybe they could find a way to go with them. There had to be a way.

CHAPTER FIFTEEN

Bagley sounded reveille at five in the morning. They had stopped during the night behind a ridge during a blinding snowstorm, and were barely able to follow the colonel's orders to park the wagons in a double line to make a windbreak. All the horses were corralled between the lines, and given oats, a rubdown, and a blanket, while the men tried to find a way to keep themselves warm for the night.

After an almost sleepless night, it took the camp less than an hour to pack up and get started. There was an air of cheerfulness amongst the men, which Rob guessed was due to the rumour of the stands of tall pines and fir trees, as well as the sweet grasses, that would give the men and animals a rest. The grass might be dry now, but would still be good grazing for the horses and oxen. There would be fresh water, as well, even if it was frozen.

Rob was doubly grateful to Pierre for sharing his wagon, and continued to cover Sam and Chris with their tent at night — much to the merriment of the rest of F Troop. Rob smiled at their jibes, but didn't stop his efforts to make Sam and Chris as comfortable as possible both day and night. Even with his care both horses' ribs showed clearly beneath the sheen of dust on their grey hides, but their plucky spirit never showed signs of wearing.

When the troopers were mounted, the colonel gave the signal to leave and the train began to move a few yards to the top of the ridge. Before F Troop reached the top, cries of wonder floated back to them, Denny ordered his horse forward and, curious, Rob and Luke followed.

The entire line ahead of them had stopped to stare at the awesome sight in the distance: mountains so tall that their tops were thrust into the clouds, which were different shades of grey. The white mountain peaks shimmered in the morning sun. Rob was too stunned to speak. Beside him, Luke was staring with his mouth hanging open.

"I wish Mum and Dad were here to see this," Rob said and Luke nodded.

They saw the mountains again and again during the three days it took to get to their camp on Milk River, which ran through the Sweet Grass Hills. It was bitterly cold. For two of those days the horses went without water except for the thin mud the thirsty animals could suck up from buffalo wallows; six of them died before reaching the camp.

Whistling and shouting at the oxen and horses, the drivers made a wide circle with the wagons to keep the horses inside and protect them from the wind. On the other side of the circle Rob saw Bagley leap down and unhitch the oxen from his wagon. He led them down to the river to drink, and Rob and Luke followed with their mounts.

"Something's up," Bagley said when the two boys joined him. "I'm not sure, but I think we're going home."

"Home?" Rob almost choked on the sip of water he had dipped from the river with his tin cup. "Home!"

Over the rim of his own cup Luke's eyes were wide.

Bagley was grinning at their surprise. "That's what I said. One of the officers let it slip that Colonel French, Colonel Macleod, Levaillee, and about four of the constables are going down to Fort Benton for supplies and to send a telegraph back East to let 'em know there's no whiskey fort out here."

"That doesn't make sense," Rob argued. "Everybody knows some of the traders use whiskey to get buffalo wolf hides from the Indians. Everybody knows that."

Bagley shrugged. "That's what I heard."

Rob turned to Luke. "Then our last chance to find where our herd's been taken is in Fort Benton. We gotta go there, too."

"We gotta," Luke echoed.

Bagley was thoughtful. "They'll probably be taking carts for the supplies they buy — not wagons. There's not much place to hide in a cart."

"I was thinking of asking Colonel Macleod," Rob said. Even as he spoke, he knew that plan was useless.

To Rob's surprise his brother had the best plan.

"The constables would be riding behind the carts," Luke pointed out. "And with most of their uniforms gone, we aren't dressed much different. Why couldn't we just ride along with them like we belonged there?"

Rob wrapped one arm around Luke's head, and rubbed his knuckles back in forth in his thick, black hair. "That's the best idea ever, Luke. I'm that tired of thinking up lies."

Luke yelped, and Rob let him go. He needed to learn more of Colonel French's plan, and think about his own.

Bagley's news turned out to be right. The next morning each troop leader announced to his men that Colonel French, along with D and E Troops, would be returning east. Along the way they would find the troopers and livestock that had been left behind and take them east as well. The troops would prepare to leave tomorrow, without Colonel French. He was going with Colonel Macleod to Fort Benton for supplies first, and three days later would join them a few miles beyond the place where the Milk River crossed the boundary line. Colonel Macleod would then return to the troops waiting at this camp and lead them farther west. Meanwhile, Inspector William Winder would be in charge.

Rob said to nothing to Luke about his own plan to go to Fort Benton, even though he knew his brother was as hopeful as he was that Smokey and at least some of the mares would be found there. It seemed almost too good to be possible, but finding them would make the difficult journey worth it.

When the officer finished speaking, the men of F Troop turned back to their usual tasks, some of them grumbling about being left behind in the wilderness. Rob beckoned for Luke to follow him to the edge of the river. For a half of an hour they sat side by side without speaking, staring at the rushing stream. When at last Rob broke the silence he tried to speak confidently and firmly, but instead found himself stumbling over his words.

"Luke, you aren't going to like what I got to say, but ... but it's something that's got to happen. You can't ... can't come with me to Fort Benton. It's going to be hard enough for just one of us to pull this off." Rob paused to plan his arguments, and was surprised to see Luke nodding his head.

"I could feel you were gonna say that, Rob. I'll stay here. I promise."

Speechless, Rob could only stare at his brother. He had expected to hear pleading, even angry words — anything but an agreement. There'd never been a time when he did anything without Luke. His was also faintly disappointed.

Sensing Rob's feelings, Luke said, "If Colonel French is going to cut northeast after he leaves Fort Benton and meet up with D and E Troops, it stands to reason that he would make us go along so's we can get home; but if I'm back here, he'd know better'n to expect you to go back without me."

Rob grabbed his brother and hugged him. He marvelled at this silent little guy, all the while wondering why he hadn't thought of that himself.

Luke turned out to be very right in his prediction.

The two boys helped Bagley hitch up his oxen. They were rested now, and had eaten the grass along the river, but you could never tell with oxen. Fed or not, rested or not, they still looked sleepy and dumb. Bagley, however, seemed fond of his team. "They'll get me where I'm going, but next time I come out here I'll be on a horse."

"You think you'll be back?" Rob asked. He liked Bagley and so did Luke. They were sorry he was leaving.

"Sure," Bagley replied. "I'm staying in the Force. They're putting men in all the Hudson's Bay posts, and they'll be setting up posts out here — probably a lot."

"Maybe you'll be in Fort Ellice," Rob said. Thinking he might see his friend again made it easier to say goodbye.

"Hope so," Bagley said. When Inspector Walker called his name he shook Luke's hand, then Rob's. "Looks like I gotta go do some bugling."

Four carts, each driven by a well armed Métis, followed two mounted officers and a scout, while four constables brought up the rear. Levaillee occasionally rode ahead to scout the land. Rob didn't know any of the constables, but as soon as they turned their horses to follow behind the carts Rob rode up to them and nodded casually. If they found it strange that someone so young was part of the group, they didn't mention it.

With the carts empty, the short train travelled quickly and by the time they camped the first night, Rob figured they had come between forty and fifty miles. He hoped the colonel would think it was too far to send him back.

They had found little water along the trail that wound through tall stands of buckbrush and dry sagebrush, so there was no need to build a fire to make tea. Instead, in the growing darkness, they sat on the dusty ground and ate pemmican and strips of dried antelope meat. Rob didn't bother trying to make himself invisible: there were too few men to hide among. When two of the constables finished their meal and sought their bedrolls it was simple for him to do the same. He fell asleep knowing it would be quite another thing to hope he remained unnoticed in the morning.

He was wrong. The men ate their morning meal while they hitched the horses and prepared to leave. Colonel French and Colonel Macleod were at the head of the line talking with Levaillee, apparently unaware that they had an extra person along. It was a dry, dusty ride, and when they paused at noon to rest the horses, Rob poured the last of the water in his canteen into his hat for Sam to drink. When she finished he wiped his hand into the creases and rubbed it across his dry, chapped mouth.

That night they camped under a small stand of scrubby trees growing beside a singing stream. The water was the best tasting Rob had ever drunk and, to make the end of the day even better, both of the colonels had been too intent on Levaillee's dirt-drawn map to take notice of him.

They started out before dawn the next morning and reached Fort Benton early in the afternoon. Looking down from the top of the hill, Rob was discouraged by what he saw. He had expected the fort to be like Fort Ellice, but even though Fort Ellice would probably fit nicely in the huge stockade about four times, this fort seemed to be made of crumbling blocks of clay instead of wood. With gaping holes in its walls, it stood about fifty yards from the widest river he had ever seen. He doubted whether he would find soldiers there that would help him get information about his horses.

Rob watched from behind one of the carts as Colonel French passed orders to the Métis to make camp where they stood, while the constables were to follow the two officers down to the town. When he saw them pass the fort and tie their mounts in front of a long, low log building he let the reins fall on Sam's neck, and she picked her way slowly down the slope. When he reached the bottom of the hill he pulled her to a halt and stared, wondering how he could go about asking people if they'd seen Smokey and the mares. Everyone seemed to be so busy. Men were rushing in and out of two long buildings carrying heavy bundles to the enormous paddle wheelers tied up beside a dock. He noticed both of the officers' horses tied in front of one of the buildings, the sign on the roof of the porch: I.C. BAKER & CO. Rob turned, instead, to a row of seven or eight smaller buildings that looked far less stable than the two stores.

Rob clicked his tongue and Sam began to move past the fort and down the street. On closer inspection, Rob saw that three of the small buildings were actually large tents with lopsided wooden frames held up by four posts, one at each corner. He could see men passing in and out of these structures — maybe men who had seen the herd. As he neared the first tent, two men staggered out and fell onto the street. Rob swung one leg over his saddle and slid to the ground, but by the time he reached them to ask if they needed help, they both were snoring lustily. The stink of whiskey floated through the air, and Rob wasn't sure if it was coming from the men or the noisy tent nearby. From another of these buildings, about hundred feet down the road, came the roar of voices raised in argument. This was followed by a single shot, which was quite enough for Rob. He wheeled his horse and cantered back up the street and went into the store across from the one the colonels had entered.

The store was small, with shelves lining the walls crowded with goods of all kinds — everything from nails to buffalo robes. Below the shelves were sacks of sugar and flour and behind a dusty glass display case Rob could see tins of tea and coffee. The prices on the cards in front astounded him: twenty dollars for a pound of coffee?

Rob had thought the store was empty, so he was startled when he turned around and saw a small middle-aged man with a long grey moustache watching him. "Help you, son?"

Blushing, Rob waited a moment to gather himself. "I don't mean to be a bother, but I didn't come to buy." He grinned. "'Specially since I got no money."

The storekeeper didn't smile back making Rob wonder if the man thought his next words would be "stick 'em up," so he quickly continued, "I been looking for a horse — a grey stallion with a silver mane and tail."

The storekeeper visibly relaxed then and walked closer to Rob. "Where'd you come from, son? On one of them paddle wheelers out there?"

"No, no. I just rode in."

The man looked puzzled. "You rode in. Where from?"

Rob wondered why they man was asking questions instead of answering his, but replied politely. "I came down from the Sweet Grass Hills with the North-West Mounted Police."

"You don't say," the storekeeper was clearly impressed. "Can't say I ever heard of the North-West Mounted Police, but they're more than welcome here, I can tell you. We're in sore need of some police work."

Four more shots rang out, punctuating his words.

The storekeeper sighed and shook his head. "To answer your question: I ain't seen a horse like that. Wish I had. But behind this store a fella named Jake runs a kind of open air stable. For a dollar he keeps horses in a corral for folks who come to town to trade and don't want their horses stolen. If there was a fancy horse, like the one you're looking for, around here he'd know it."

CHAPTER SIXTEEN

A corral! What better place to find the herd! Rob's first instinct was to run through the weeds to the back of the store, but he realized that a horse with thin streaks of silver in her mane and tail might attract notice if he left her behind — and Colonel Macleod was right across the street. He untied Sam from the hitching post in front of the store, and led her around to the back of the building to the corral, which was holding about a dozen horses. There was no sign of Smokey or the mares. Swallowing his disappointment wasn't too difficult: he'd done it so many times already he was becoming accustomed to it.

A thin man sat, arms folded across his chest, tilting his chair back against a lean-to. He wore a wide-brimmed black hat pulled down over his eyes; below it the ends of a thick, grey moustache blended into a full beard of the same colour. His chin was on his chest, and he appeared to be sleeping. Hoping not to startle the old man, Rob tied his own horse to a post and moved toward the man quietly.

"Say, mister," Rob froze: the man shot to his feet, a six shooter in his hand.

Flinty blue eyes looked Rob up and down. Apparently satisfied with what he saw, the man put his gun away and sat down. "What can I do for ya, son?"

Too shocked to speak for a moment, Rob gulped twice and replied, "I was told you might know something ... I mean, the storekeeper back there said I was to ask you if you saw a horse I'm missing."

The man seemed confused so Rob forced himself to relax and speak slowly, "I'm looking for a horse — a stallion and maybe some mares with him."

"These horses — they belong to you?"

Encouraged, since the horse-keeper didn't say no, Rob's words rushed out. Without planning to, he told the whole story of losing the herd and his trek with the North-West Mounted Police. When he finished he stood waiting — hope in his eyes.

Finally the old timer said, "I been thinking. Know I ain't seen a horse like your Smokey — sure would remember him if I did. However, about three months back a feller rode in on a fine looking grey mare. I recall he was showing her to some buyer off one of the ships. Seems like he was bragging about how powerful she was, and that he had more where she came from."

Rob went cold. His biggest fear had been learning that the herd had been sold and taken south where they'd never find them. He forced himself to ask, "Did he sell them?

"Not as far as I can tell, and I'm right here day and night." He gestured at the lean-to behind the store. "Don't think the buyer was interested in horses, and I don't expect there's none around here that wants to pay fancy prices for a horse. Most folks catch 'em wild and break 'em."

Rob thanked the horse-keeper and left. Ready for the angry lecture he was sure to get from Colonel French, Rob squared his shoulders and led Sam across the wide, dusty road to I. C. Baker & Co.

Inside the larger store, the trade goods were stacked neatly in piles on the shelves and floor. Rob looked around amazed at the variety of goods that had been brought upriver. Far behind the long counter that ran the entire length of the room were vegetables and fruits, both fresh and dried, separated into bins. Rob had seen potatoes and cabbages before, harvested from Mum's garden. And their two apple trees produced plenty of fruit, some dried for winter like the ones here in glass jars, but he only had seen the golden, round oranges in books. His mouth began to water.

There were more than a dozen customers demanding attention from the two busy clerks, but no sign of Colonel Macleod or Colonel French. Rob wasn't expecting to see any of the constables: he had spotted them watching the workers bustling around the paddle wheelers. As he turned to leave, a door opened at the far end of the room and the two colonels came out, still listening to a neatly dressed man who towered above them both. "Send down your carts. I'll have them loaded and on the way to your camp by daybreak," he was saying.

As the three men were shaking hands, the door opened and a short man dressed in buckskins walked in carrying a Winchester rifle more than half as tall as he was. He looked like the goose eggs Rob and Luke had gathered in the spring, except this egg had a head and two bowed legs. He wanted to laugh, but there was something about the calm face and dark, deep-set eyes that stopped him.

"Here he is now," the storekeeper said gesturing for the man to come over. Rob watched Colonel French's face as he surveyed the newcomer from the high-topped moccasin boots on his feet to the dusty, black bowler hat on his head. The officer's face betrayed nothing as they were introduced, but Rob sensed that he wasn't impressed. The three men walked up to the door, passing Rob before they reached it. Each of the officers gave Rob a silent, level stare.

Outside Rob found Colonel Macleod standing by his horse. He moved toward him, wondering what he was going to say. He was sick of apologizing, but even so he began, "I know you're plenty tired of seeing me sneaking around, sir, but I...."

"Too late for apologies, lad," the colonel interrupted. "Best you go up hill to our camp. We'll be along after Colonel French receives the reply to his telegram."

"Yes sir," Rob said and started across the street to get his horse, but Colonel Macleod ordered him to stop. When he turned, he found the officer extending his hand. He was holding one of the golden oranges Rob had seen inside. Struck dumb, Rob stared at the colonel.

"Take it," the officer said and thrust it into Rob's hand. "It will do you good."

Rob grinned from ear to ear. "Thank you, sir. I'll keep it until we get back to the Hills. I want to share it with Luke."

"No need. I have another one for Luke."

The tall storekeeper had kept his word. The carts were loaded with boots, blankets, oats .... everything, Rob figured, that the troops at Sweet Grass Hills needed. As he watched the carts appear over the top of the hill,

Rob worried about the state of Luke's boots. Stuffing dried grass into them to cover the holes in the soles didn't help keep the cold out. His own were no better, but he wasn't coughing like Luke.

Not far behind the carts, twelve oxen were struggling up the hill in teams of six — each team pulling a towering canvas covered load lashed to the wagon bed. Rob was amazed that the top-heavy vehicles didn't tip over. They were accompanied by three men on horseback, one of whom was the storekeeper from Fort Benton.

When both wagons reached the top they came to a halt, and the storekeeper slid off his horse. He dusted off his clothing as he walked over to greet Colonel French, who was standing with the rest of his officers in front of his tent. They also looked surprised. Rob didn't bother trying to hide his eaves dropping when Colonel French offered his hand to the man and said, "Well, Mr. Conrad, sir, I did not expect to see you again so soon."

Mr. Conrad grinned and said, "Nor did I, Colonel. It came to me late last night when I recalled that you intend to build a fort not far over the line. I think it would be good for me to set up a store for Mounties and Indians alike near that spot. Meanwhile," he gestured toward his wagons and added, "we can do business from the wagons."

Colonel French's face crinkled at the word "Mounties." He looked like he'd found a bug in his breakfast and Rob stifled a snicker.

The officer recovered quickly, and offered Mr. Conrad his hand. "That's a capital plan, sir, and one Colonel Macleod and his men will appreciate."

Colonel Macleod's serious face was lit up by his grin. "Truly, this will make life a bit easier for the men. Even though you had contracted to bring supplies to us, having the store nearby will be, well, it will be a pleasure."

"No doubt we will be seeing a good bit of each other in the future," Mr. Conrad said. "I hope you play chess, Colonel Macleod."

Before the train of men and goods separated — Colonel French to go northeast to the boundary line to join his troops, and Colonel Macleod back to Sweet Grass Hills — Rob was told to go speak with the commanding officer. Although he was apprehensive of the tongue-lashing he knew he would get, Rob was bolstered by the knowledge that in a day or two he would rejoin Luke. He couldn't wait to tell him their herd hadn't been taken down the Missouri River.

The line of carts and wagons had halted, and Colonel French was bidding goodbye to Mr. Conrad and Colonel Macleod. When they rode back to their place at the head of their wagons, Colonel French looked at Rob. "This time, young man, you have no choice. You are going back to Roche Percée with me, and from there you will be accompanied to Fort Ellice."

Rob was stunned. "But, sir, I can't. I just can't. Thank you, but...."

Colonel French held up his hand to stop the flow of protests. "You can't?"

Rob's words came tumbling out. "I appreciate you wanting ... I — I can't go back with you, sir. My brother Luke is up at the Hills. I got to look after him. I ..."

Rob was astonished to see a smile lift the corners of the officer's mouth. "I tried," he said. "Go along then." As Rob backed Sam away, the colonel added, "Rob, in a year or two, you might consider joining our force. We could use you." With that he raised his hand and swept it forward; his line began to move.

When they made camp that night Rob found Colonel Macleod alone for once and told him what Colonel French had said. The officer smiled. "Aye, Rob, let that be a lesson for you never to judge a man too soon. But I'm pleased that you told me, for it reminds of what the colonel asked me to do. I'll be but a moment."

Rob waited as Colonel Macleod walked a few paces to one of the carts. He returned with a pair of tall leather moccasins and a buffalo coat and dumped them in Rob's arms. "Colonel French chose these for you himself, Rob, knowing it would take a team of horses he couldn't spare to drag you back to Fort Ellice without your brother."

CHAPTER SEVENTEEN

With the carts loaded and the addition of the two heavily loaded wagons, it took an extra two days to reach the camp in the Sweet Grass Hills and another day to get to the new camp. Rob was excited to be invited to ride ahead with Colonel Macleod. The officer had explained that in Fort Benton he'd learned there was a far better place to camp fifteen miles west, where they would find sheltering trees, water, and good hunting. He sent word for the camp to move there.

What was even more interesting was learning that they had been camped less than fifty miles from the ill-famed Fort Whoop-Up! Potts, their new scout, had said that even had they known they were so close, they wouldn't have found any whiskey traders. News had spread of the arrival of a police force and, added to that, the trading season was over.

It was late afternoon when they arrived at the new camp, where they were greeted by Inspector Winder and everyone in camp. From Sam's back, Rob scanned the noisy mob of men, trying to see Luke, with no success. He trotted his horse through the camp to find him. Images of Luke being too ill to come out of the tent filled his mind, and finally he swung from his saddle and approached Inspector Winder, who was deep in conversation with Colonel Macleod. "Excuse me, sir," he began, and waited for the man to turn to him.

The look in Winder's eyes made Rob's heart plummet with fear. "Rob, I'm sorry that you must hear bad news the moment you get here. I'm afraid Luke is missing, along with Inspector Denny."

"Missing?" Rob croaked.

"For how long?" asked Colonel Macleod.

"Since yesterday," the officer replied. "I'm told they went hunting together early in the morning, and haven't yet returned. We fired the cannon once and almost lost three more horses; so I didn't dare fire it again."

Rob still couldn't speak, but Colonel Macleod asked the questions he couldn't bring himself to ask. "Have they been searched for?"

"Of course, sir. At least a dozen of the men volunteered to look for them, but most are back now."

Rob's mind was working now. "Did they tell anyone which way they were going?"

Winder nodded. "They started off going east to look for antelope, and some of the men tracked them almost ten miles that way, but when they turned north the trail disappeared."

Rob thanked the officer and led Sam away to look down the line of tents for his own round-topped one. *Anything could have happened to them. Indians maybe. Or one of the wildcats that some say hang in the trees waiting to jump on whatever looks good to eat. No, better to think their horses played out and they're walking.* Rob shook his head, knowing that Luke's horse wouldn't give up. He felt a tiny wave of annoyance when he heard footsteps following behind; he wanted to be alone to think.

A hand touched his shoulder, and he turned to see the funny looking guide that Colonel Macleod had hired in Fort Benton.

"Brother lost." It was neither a question nor a statement, but something in between.

Rob nodded.

"Come. We'll go take a look."

It didn't occur to Rob to question him. Two were better than one anytime, and he was very uncertain about where to start looking for his brother. Without a word, leading Sam, he followed Potts to where he had tied his horse. Both animals still had their packs tied behind the saddles.

As they trotted away from the camp, Rob had a sudden thought. "Wait, Mr. Potts. I think I better tell Colonel Macleod or somebody that we're going out to look for Luke."

Without slowing, Potts replied, "Told 'em."

On the ride from Fort Benton Rob had already learned that the scout spoke very little. He also learned that when he did speak, men listened. Rob hid a grin when when, after a long period of silence, his companion said, "No Mr. Potts — name's Bear Child." Then with a twinkle in his dark eyes he said, "Call me Potts."

Rob studied the man as the horses kept up a fast walk. He was uneasy when he noticed that Potts didn't seem to be looking at the ground for signs, but he reminded himself that Mr. Conrad had said there was no man better at tracking. When they camped on the way back from Fort Benton, Conrad had filled him in on Potts's story.

"He's about thirty-five or thirty-six, from what I hear," the storekeeper had said. "A bit on the young side to be a widely know legend. His father was a Scottish trader and his mother was from the Blood tribe. Jerry was just a tyke when his father was killed at the fort where they lived. It was a long way southwest of here on the Missouri."

Colonel Macleod had commented on Potts' age. "I would have taken him for a bit older than thirty-five. There's something in his eyes...." The officer's voice trailed away, and he stood, straightening his jacket. "I fear I'm becoming fanciful."

"Not at all," Conrad smiled ruefully. "I think you said it right. There's a lot of memories behind those eyes — some good, and some very bad."

The colonel sat again and reached out his hands to the fire. "Did his mother go back to her tribe?"

"I understand that she did, but she left Potts at the fort. It's said that she wanted her son to learn the ways of his father's people; but she came back often to visit him; and sometimes he went with her to stay in her village."

"So he's neither fish nor fowl," the colonel joked.

Conrad shook his head slowly. "I'd say he's a good bit more than that — rather that he is a good combination. His mother was wise to leave him at the fort. There were some hard men there, but he was more or less adopted by one of the factors, who gave him a basic education — reading, sums, writing. His mother's people taught him the ways of the land."

Rob had wondered then about the scout's mother, and in a break in the conversation he asked, "Does Potts still go back to his tribe? Is his mother still alive?"

Conrad hesitated, then said, "No, she's not alive, Rob. Her village had been quite a large one, but there were disagreements among the people, which divided it almost in half. Potts's mother was senselessly shot and killed one night several years ago. Jerry had grown up and left the area before that happened, but when he learned of it he found the man who did it and shot him." He glanced at Colonel Macleod and added, "Perhaps that's one of the things you see behind his eyes."

Rob's thoughts flew back to the present as Potts turned his horse northward and bent to scan the ground. Rob looked down, too, but he saw nothing other than sand-coloured dirt interspersed between clumps of dried sagebrush that were casting shadows. Rob bit his lip. Dusk was approaching, and soon it would be too dark for even the best of trackers to see. Still, they moved slowly and steadily for four more miles before Potts halted his horse and jumped to the ground beside a tiny rivulet. When he pulled his pack from behind his saddle and dropped it on the ground, Rob figured they would be camping there. Without a word, he slid from his saddle and led both horses to drink from the clear, fresh stream. When they finished, he stripped off their saddles and placed them near one of the scrubby looking trees that was growing a few feet from the water. After removing Sam's bridle, he rubbed her down with the blanket and turned her loose. He did the same for the scout's brown mare, and raised his eyebrows at Potts. Potts responded. "She won't stray."

The scout had built a tiny fire, and they took turns drinking from the wide cup in which he had made tea. Rob wished he had something to contribute to their supper, but he only had pemmican in his pack left over from his return from Fort Benton, an amount about equal to what Potts also had. They had no tent, and the ground was cold under the blanket he'd spread out, but Rob managed to fall asleep. He sensed that the care he'd taken of the horses had given him acceptance in Potts's eyes.

He slept fitfully on the cold ground with only two rough blankets for cover. When he heard Potts stirring at daybreak, Rob rose and stretched his stiff muscles. After some more tea and a handful of pemmican, he felt a little better, even more so when Potts said, "Today we find 'em."

Knowing how hard the disappointment would be if Potts were wrong, Rob tried not to count too heavily on what he had said; but he quickly got ready. Potts seemed to be scanning the ground closely and they rode more slowly this time. When the sun rose higher in the sky, Rob turned to look back. The previous night the

Sweet Grass Hills had been a big purple bump in the distance, and now, except for an occasional low, rolling hill, the prairie was flat in every direction. Rob figured he could see for miles, and nowhere was there a sign of a human or a horse.

CHAPTER EIGHTEEN

It was an effort to keep from asking Potts if he knew where they were headed. He didn't have to wonder long. Twice the scout had dismounted and led his horse through the short wild grass, browned now and brittle. The second time he did so, he jumped back on his horse and with a clicking sound from his lips, she cantered forward and Rob followed in his tracks.

Less than a half a mile ahead, Rob could see that there was a break in the flat prairie as though the grass and bush had been parted. Potts' horse leaped forward and Sam followed. They paused on the top of a ridge and looked down at the wide coulee that stretched along a fair sized river. Rob gasped at what he saw.

Below him and on the steep hillside across the water were giant rocks thrust up from the hard packed cracked earth — some were like near Roche Percée, only twisted and weird like frozen apparitions. There were willows along the narrow river, dead leaves clinging to their branches and, farther away, Rob recognized masses of chokecherry bushes among other shrubs crowded against the huge stones. Some of these still wore green leaves. He started when he felt a hand touch his sleeve.

Potts was pointing to the sky. "Storm's comin'. Be over quick."

Rob looked upward to see a mass of low black clouds moving toward them at a fast rate. The air had suddenly grown colder but he was comfortable inside his new warm coat and boots. He wished he'd brought along the boots and buffalo jacket that Colonel Macleod had waiting for Luke back at the camp.

Without being told, Sam followed Potts' horse as it walked along the top the hill. Rob realized the scout was looking for a way down. *If I had a choice, I'd as soon flatten myself against a bush on the prairie as I would to go down to those spooky statues.* Rob said to himself. A moment later he changed his mind. *But what if that's where Luke and Denny are? Nah, They'd have more sense. You could get lost down there.*

By the time Rob finished his conversation with himself, Potts had found a zigzag trail and started downward.

Gripping his knees hard into Sam's flanks, he let her find her way on the twists and turns. At the bottom Potts wasted no time searching for shelter. The sky had grown dark and the light breeze had quickened to a strong wind. It was cold enough to snow; but the first drops that fell were water. They swiftly grew into large, round pellets of ice that bounced off the rocks around them like ricocheting bullets.

The hail turned to sleet that, whipped by the wind, made it almost impossible for Rob to see Potts riding ahead of him through the twists and turns around the tall rocks. Sam stopped suddenly, bumping into the rear of Potts' mount, and Rob felt a hand on his arm. "Here," Potts shouted, pointing to one of the rocks. It protruded from the hillside, leaving a wide space underneath — room enough for the two of them and the horses if they stood sideways in the shelter.

Out of the storm, Rob felt fairly warm and dry — except for his trousers. They and his moccasins were soaked, but the buffalo coat had repelled the sleet and hail. He looked at Potts who wore only the buckskins and boots that he had on when they left Fort Benton. If the scout was cold and wet, he didn't show it, except for taking off his odd looking hat and shaking the water from it. He sat down motioning for Rob to do the same.

"Won't last," he said pointing west to a sliver of blue showing through the dark clouds. "Here we find your brother."

Potts was right: the storm ended just as suddenly as it had begun, leaving streams of sandy water trickling down the hillsides. It collected between the rocks, forming a shallow rivulet for the horses to splash through as they continued to walk through the forest of rocks. Rob's heart sank when he realized that the storm would have obliterated any tracks they might have found, if Luke and Denny were in this canyon. Worry for Luke gave him the courage to question the scout.

"Potts, I was wondering…." His words trailed away as he realized his question was foolish.

Potts had been looking straight ahead. He turned now, and replied as though he had read Rob's mind. "Son," he said gesturing upward. "There's not been any tracks for the past six miles. We keep looking."

The sun rose higher and from its warmth steam curled upward from some of the rocks, adding to their ghostly appearance. They stopped often to climb the rocks and look around for any sign of men or horses. "Why don't we just yell and see if they answer?" Rob suggested. But Potts's reply only gave him one more thing to worry about.

"Maybe some enemies in here."

Rob had no idea how far they had come, picking their way in the shadows of the rocks, but when Potts declared it was time to rest the horses, he was glad to slide down from his saddle. He stood stretching and watched Potts clamber through the twisted shapes before climbing one to look around. Seconds later he was sliding down. Rob, too, had heard the clip-clop of shod hoofs. By the time Potts reached the ground, the horse was there.

"Look, Potts," Rob said excitedly, "It's Denny's horse. I can tell by the saddle: it's marked like all the police horses."

Potts' expressionless face showed no excitement, but his words made Rob's heart leap with hope. "It is time to call you brother. Be loud."

Luke's name bounced off the rocks and back again. Rob cried out three times, each time waiting, without success, for his own name to be echoed in response. "Keep trying," Potts ordered.

Rob's straining throat was sore and his words had gone raspy before Potts held up his hand for silence. Then he heard it — a faint echo in the distance. He and Potts mounted their horses and, leading Denny's animal, they moved further into the maze of sandstones.

Luke and Denny were closer than their voices had indicated. Rob's heart was almost too full to speak when a quick survey of his brother revealed that he appeared to be all right, and so was Denny.

After happy greetings and hand shakings, the inspector was quick to explain why they hadn't returned to camp. "I seem to have a penchant for horse trouble. I winged an antelope yesterday in the afternoon, and we trailed it in here." He paused and looked around. "Interesting spot, eh? I lost the trail after a rattler took aim at my horse. She shied and I went over her head. When I awoke, she had disappeared and, happily, so had the snake."

"Where were you, Luke?" Rob asked.

It was Denny who replied. "Luke had gone on ahead to find a way to climb higher and find a way out of here. He returned to find me lying senseless. Stupid of me."

"I tracked the horse, Rob," Luke said, "but there were too many ways she could go. Guess I picked the wrong one."

"You did just fine," the inspector said firmly.

"Where'd you spend the night?" Rob asked.

"In the rocks," Denny said. "They were still marvellously warm from the sun."

"I think we would've found the horse today if it didn't storm," Luke said.

It was then that Rob realized his brother's jacket was still wet and he was trying to hide a cough. Stripping off his buffalo coat, Rob handed it to Luke. "You put this on." Over Luke's protests, he said, "What's Mum going to say if you get pneumonia?"

Watching them, Denny said, "Rob's right, but first we should try making a fire. I have just enough tea left for four. We'll have to figure out how to get out of this place and back to the Hills. I confess to being totally lost: all the prairie above here looks exactly the same."

Rob glanced at Potts and saw his moustache twitch with a fleeting grin, but his eyes were dead serious when spoke. Pointing over his shoulder, he said, "See those pictures scratched on the rocks? This is a sacred place for most tribes — for sure Blackfoot. They find us here, they won't ask questions."

"Never mind the tea for now," Denny said, scrambling onto his horse. "But I hope you will join me in a cup back at camp." He glanced upward, and Rob heard him mutter softly, "If we find our way back."

Now that Luke and Denny had been found, Rob had no worries for the present. Riding behind his brother as they followed Potts on the winding path through the rocks, he was confident the amazing scout would lead them to the Hills. In less than an hour they were at the bottom of the cliff that he and Potts had ridden down. With the scout's order, they dismounted to lead the horses up the twisted path he had chosen.

"There now, you see," Denny said almost triumphantly as he swept his arm in a wide arc to cover the vast nothingness on the brown prairie.

Potts didn't hesitate. He turned his horse and pointed ahead. "Southwest."

Their horses side by side now, Rob was eager to tell Luke about his trip to Fort Benton. "You should've seen it, Luke. A lot of shacks, but there's two stores and the paddle wheelers coming and going."

"But not our horses?" Luke asked.

"No, but that's good thing. Now we know they have to be someplace where Dad can look. I've got it figured that with the police keeping an eye out for them and spreading the word at the forts, somebody will see them. The wolfers can't keep the herd hid forever."

Luke nodded, and Rob went on to tell his brother about the boots and buffalo coat that were waiting for him back in camp. "Good." Luke said. If he said anything else, it was cut off when Denny, who had been riding beside Potts, dropped back to ride beside Rob.

"Do you know anything about those animal pictures on the rocks back there? I tried to ask Potts how long they have been there and who made them; but he doesn't seem to have much to say."

"He doesn't talk much," Rob agreed. "Maybe one of the Métis drivers knows something about them."

Luke had ridden up ahead to join Potts, who now seemed to be talking quite a bit. Scarcely listening to what Denny had to say, Rob watched with growing unease and a sense of resentment. After all, he had come to search for his brother and given him his coat and there he was chattering like a squirrel to somebody he didn't even know. That was the strange part. Rob thought back to when Luke was little. *Once he got past looking for his mum and learned the white man's way of talking he was a pretty happy little kid. He played and hooted and hollered just like I did. Funny, though, how he started to change a while back — quieter, sort of, and not talking much. Oh, he'd answer politely enough when Mum and Dad talked to him, and he never really stopped talking to me, but he seems to be turning in on himself like he's got a secret hid inside. Seems plenty strange how he's hitting it off with Potts.*

Denny was still talking, and Rob looked over at him hoping the man hadn't noticed his lack of attention. It wouldn't have mattered. A hazy dark cloud was appearing on the horizon straight ahead. Rob groaned — not another hailstorm. Potts pushed his mount to a canter, and the rest of them followed. They were still miles away when the shape gradually became a purplish blue, and lower versions spread beside it.

"Sweet Grass Hills!" Rob shouted.

CHAPTER NINETEEN

Rob thought the entire camp must have turned out to welcome them back. While he and his companions were still on their horses, some of the of the troopers fired questions. They were mostly for Denny, who would say nothing until he had publicly thanked Jerry Potts. The poker-faced scout waved away the thanks and slid to the ground. He busied himself stripping the saddle from his horse and leading her to water.

Knowing Denny would tell their tale better than they could, Rob beckoned to Luke and they rode down to their tent. "Better get out of those wet clothes, Luke," Rob advised. "I'll see to the horses." He found it strange that Luke didn't protest, but lifted the tent flap and disappeared inside.

He was becoming increasingly worried about Luke, so he watered their horses quickly and hurried them back to the tent before removing their saddles and rubbing them down. That done, Rob entered the tent to find Luke, still in his wet clothes, stretched on a blanket, sleeping soundly. Certain he must be hungry, Rob started to lean down to wake his brother, but knelt instead to pull off the tattered, wet boots and damp trousers. Luke started to mutter in his sleep, and Rob moved closer to him, bending to listen. It was then that he felt the heat rising from his brother. Fever! A bad one. He rose and looked around. Luke was still wearing the buffalo coat, but his legs and feet were bare. Snatching up his own pair of blankets, Rob tucked one around Luke's legs and covered him with the other. Unable to ignore the pain of hunger in his belly, he left the tent to find something to eat.

Although lately there had been no lack of meat, there had been no bread and little tea for some time. There were half a dozen fires, each with a man designated to cook up the supplies that had been brought from Fort Benton. For his meeting with these men, Mr. Conrad added enough luxuries to made every man in the camp his friend for life. Besides tins of tea, Rob spied sugar, canned beans, canned peaches, and small, sweet biscuits. His mouth watered.

The men of C Troop hailed Rob over to join them, and he didn't hesitate. He rummaged inside the wagon and found his plate. He filled it twice with antelope and beans before helping himself to peaches and two of the biscuits. Finished, he rolled his eyes blissfully and rubbed his stomach. "I don't think anything ever tasted so good to me," he said, and the men around the fire erupted with laughter.

Colonel Macleod had been walking down the line of campfires speaking with the men around them. When he reached F Troop, he told them, "I want every man who is unwell to make himself known to the officer in charge of his troop. We will be moving out in two days to find Fort Whoop-Up and the men that savagely killed all the people in a village camped nearby. There's no telling what we might come upon and, in a fight, it would dangerous for everyone if we were bringing sick men."

There was a chorus of "yes sirs" and "thank you sirs" before the officer turned to leave. Rob stood and said, "Sir, does that mean Luke and me have to stay behind?"

The colonel looked at Rob up and down. "Why do you ask? Are you sick?"

"No, sir," Rob replied, "but I think Luke is. He's been sneezing and coughing for a long while, and now he has a fever as well."

Colonel Macleod sighed. "Come along then. Best I have a look at him."

When he entered the tent the colonel sniffed the air and said, "He has fever. That's certain." He looked down at Luke for some time, and said, "I wish I had something to give to him. Before he left, Dr. Kittson gave me some laudanum for any man who becomes injured, but I have nothing for fever."

Thinking out loud, Rob said, "Mum likely would say to keep him warm and give him a lot of water."

The colonel pushed his hat to the back of his head and stood staring down at Luke. "Probably good advice," he muttered. To Rob's surprise, the man leaned down and scooped Luke up in his arms. To Rob he said, "Sleeping with only a blanket to keep him from the cold ground won't help him. We'll put him in Pierre's wagon." Rob ran to hold open the tent flap and, with Luke in his arms, the officer ducked his head to go out. With a perfectly straight face, Macleod said, "Perhaps there is a bed there already."

Rob felt his face turn red. Like Colonel French, this commanding officer knew everything that went on in his camp.

Luke slept until evening the following day and, to Rob, he looked as though he felt better, though his face was still flushed with fever. Rob had felt a thrill of fear run up his spine the night before when Colonel Macleod crawled into the wagon carrying a cup of fresh water, just as he had the night before McDuff died.

Rob felt sick himself when he realized he and Luke would be staying behind with the men who were ill. He wanted more than anything to get to Fort Whoop-Up and see if the horses were there. It was his last hope of finding them. But he didn't have to be reminded that his first duty was looking after his brother. He wanted to jump up and down with joy when he later learned he and Luke would be going on with the rest of the troops; he could hardly believe his good luck. It was Denny who ordered the driver of their wagon to line up with B Troop.

Without a trace of resentment, Denny said to Rob, "Colonel Macleod's orders. I suspect he believes he will fare better with him watching over Luke."

For a moment, Rob searched for words to comfort Denny: he knew how much the inspector had wanted to be in on the fight for Fort Whoop-Up.

The B and C Troops moved out early the next morning, and stopped frequently to rest the horses before they camped that night. Everyone was impressed with Potts's abilities. He guided them to a well-travelled trail, which was so rutted they only advanced ten miles. Satisfied that they would stay on the trail, he had gone on ahead.

There were whispers in the line of men when the scout disappeared. "Remember that Morrow? He was a spy hired by the whiskey traders to keep us away from their fort, for sure. What if Potts is the same?" The mood changed in the late afternoon when Potts was seen cooking meat at a campfire beside Milk River. A large cleaned and dressed buffalo lay on a long, flat rock nearby.

Colonel Macleod had brought only one of the nine pound cannons, but, as usual, it slowed their progress. Rob had heard Potts telling the colonel that they wouldn't need it: "No need for the gun. Whiskey traders left."

Each time the colonel had patiently replied. "I have my orders, Jerry. I have no choice."

Rob was torn between relief that the troopers might not have to fight, and disappointment. *If the whiskey traders aren't there, that means the horses won't be there either. But ... the ones that stole our herd are wolfers. Maybe they're both — whiskey traders and wolfers, too.* He shook his head.

Bagley wasn't there to blow reveille, but the camp was roused at dawn by the raucous cries of the ravens, which began as the first streaks of light moved across the sky. In the wagon bed, Rob rolled on his side to peer at his brother and was surprised to see Luke, eyes wide open, staring back at him. Rob sat up. "How do you feel, Luke?"

His reply was a hoarse whisper. "Good. I feel good."

Rob was stern. "You know what Mum says about telling stories, so quit fibbing, or I won't give you the orange the colonel bought for you."

Luke's eyes brightened for an instant, but they faded again when he said, "Don't matter, Rob. Nothing you can do about it."

"Maybe so, maybe not, but I'm your brother and I want to know how you're doing."

Luke sighed and pointed to his chest. "It hurts here, and I'm cold clear through to my bones."

Rob was immediately angry at himself. He should have put both buffalo coats on Luke instead of keeping one for himself. He got to his knees and began to pull his off.

"I don't want your coat, Rob. I want to sit by the fire before we get started again."

"Sure. Be right back," Rob said, jumping from the wagon. The air was crisp and cold, but there was no wind. They had camped on a small, flat mesa without water, but there was plenty, for the horses and for tea, in the barrels they were carrying. Campfires were already flickering to life, and there was the murmur of voices as men moved out of their tents. Rob reached into the back of the wagon for two tin cups in the corner and went over to the nearest campfire. He had spent most of the journey with F Troop, so Rob didn't know some of the troops he was now travelling with. The constable tending the fire was as red-haired as himself, and Rob heard that his name was Bruce. Whether it was first or last, he wasn't sure.

The trooper looked up with a cheery grin. "I'm guessing you're here for your tea, lad. Help yourself, there's plenty. The menu for this morning is buffalo and biscuits. I'll be making them meself."

In spite of his concern for Luke, Rob found his spirits lift. "Sounds good. I'll take you up on that tea in a minute. My brother's sick, and I'm going to bring him out by the fire. After that I can help you."

The constable waved his hand and replied, "Not at all, at all, Rob. You just tend to Luke. I can manage fine."

I don't know him, but he seems to know us, Rob thought as he put the two cups on the ground near the fire and returned to Luke. *Strange.*

Although there were very few supplies in the wagon, it was cramped quarters and Rob struggled to get Luke warmly dressed and out of the wagon. Rob jumped out, and Luke leaned on him heavily as he climbed over the wheel. Together they went to the fire, where Rob was once again touched by the goodness of the men: a flat rock had been pushed closer to the warmth of the fire and Luke was told to sit there.

The biscuits were surprising good, and Rob ate four; but Luke took only one mouthful before nibbling at his one. He didn't touch the strip of antelope in his hand. Instead he sat nodding with his eyes closed.

Rob watched his brother, his heart heavy, wondering what he could do to help Luke get well. The sound of raised voices ahead in the line of fires interrupted his thoughts, and he stood to see better. Seven Native men had walked into the camp carrying rifles. Colonel Macleod was striding toward them, his hand outstretched. Rob saw Jerry Potts moving easily beside him.

When Rob stood to see better, the red-haired trooper gestured toward the group and said to Rob, "Why don't you go see what's up."

With a glance at his dozing brother, Rob trotted over to where the colonel and Potts were meeting the natives. A tall, bony-faced man with greying hair held up his hand in greeting, and the colonel raised his in response. All was quiet as the man spoke in a deep voice, often sweeping one arm in a wide circle, gesturing with his hands. The words flowed from his lips. Rob wished he could understand what he was saying, so he appreciated the colonel's request for Potts to translate.

Potts had been listening carefully, and he turned to Colonel Macleod and said, "He says you are welcome here."

Colonel Macleod's eyebrows shot up. "That's all?"

Potts nodded. "Better the speaker: longer the talk." Quietly, he added, "They're Blackfoot."

The elder began speaking again, and this time Potts said, "He wants a sit-down talk, and for you to smoke a pipe with him and his people. He says a bunch of them are over the hill." He pointed to a rise above their campsite. "Might be good to ask them over."

Colonel Macleod took a deep breath, and nodded his head. "If you think it best."

Before the hour ended, about thirty male Blackfoot and three times that many women and children appeared on the hill. They were very quiet. Seven of the men — all dignified looking elders — sat cross-legged on the ground, while the rest of the group stood far behind. With a whispered word from the scout, Colonel Macleod, Inspectors Brisebois and Winder, and Potts approached them and sat down opposite. The pipe was lit and passed carefully from one man to the next in the seated circle.

When the speeches began Rob returned to the fire. Luke was still dozing, sitting up. After listening to Rob's report, the rest of the men went over to see the spectacle. Rob looked at Luke carefully. His normally copper-coloured skin was still a blotchy rose colour. Rob sighed, wishing he knew what to do to break the fever. He spun around when he heard the rustling of dried grass behind him. He could see nothing. Bending over, he found a fat stick and threw it into the fire. Sparks flew, and Luke jerked awake. "What is it?" he asked thickly.

Before Rob could answer, he saw two figures out of the corner of his eye. A tall, slim Native lad stood with his arms folded across his chest, and a small Native girl stood at his side. Rob was struck by her beauty and her graceful movements as she moved closer to him. Her thick, dark hair was parted neatly in the middle and hung in one long braid down her back. Her face was heart shaped, and over raised cheekbones, her thickly lashed brown eyes laughed as she looked at him.

Rob stumbled to his feet. "Uh — hello," he said. The boy said nothing, but the girl looked at him, her eyebrows raised high.

He tried again. "Good morning."

This time the boy shrugged and frowned, but the girl stepped closer to Luke. She looked at Rob questioningly, then cautiously put a hand to Luke's face. She drew it back, and spoke quickly to the youth. Together they disappeared.

Rob wished he knew what was going on.

Colonel Macleod and Potts were still deep in discussions with the Blackfoot men when, less than an hour later, the girl reappeared with a hunched old woman. Rob thought the woman must be at least a hundred years old. She had no visible teeth, and above her wrinkled face, thin grey hair hung on her forehead. She was carrying a deep, wooden bowl filled with a murky liquid. When she brought it close to Luke, Rob stood to protest, but the girl laid a hand on his arm and shook her head.

Rob stared at the crone as she brought the bowl up to Luke's face; he didn't object when she gently pushed it against his lips, forcing him to drink. With the first swallow his face twisted in disgust, and Rob thought he was going to spit out the liquid. Again the old woman pushed the bowl against his mouth. Luke kept swallowing until it was empty. With the girl supporting her, the old woman limped away.

Luke looked at Rob and muttered hoarsely, "Worst tea I ever had."

"I feel like a fool, Luke," Rob said, staring into the last embers of the fire. "I don't know what to do to help you get over this, and then I let some...." He didn't know how to finish his thought.

"I know," Luke responded. He staggered to his feet. "I think I'd like to go back to sleep."

When he had his brother tucked warmly on the bed of the wagon, Rob went to join the rest of the police who were trying to listen to the discussion between Colonel Macleod and the chief. The red-haired constable noticed him and said in a low tone, "We're staying here again tonight. Potts said this could be a long powwow."

Potts was right. The sun had already risen high and was starting its descent, and still the conference went on. Rob made sure to check on Luke throughout the day. When he went to the wagon again, in the late afternoon, he was startled to see Luke sitting up, the flush gone from his face and his eyes clear and bright. "Howdy," he said with a small grin.

Rob vaulted into the wagon and put a hand on his brother's cheek. It was cool. "Hey, Luke, I think your fever's gone!"

"I don't know, maybe. My chest doesn't hurt so much anymore, and I'm not coughing a lot." He inched forward to the end of the wagon. "I'm starving. Is there anything left to eat?"

Rob was so relieved, that goosebumps rose to cover his arms. Luke's steps were wobbly, but he was quick to reach the campfire and snatch another biscuit and a strip of meat. Mouth full, he said, "This tastes goooood!"

Rob laughed. "Luke, did you think that tea you had from the Indian woman made you better?"

Luke took a deep breath and blew it out noisily. "Figure it must, because it tasted even worse than the stuff Mum gives us."

"Wonder what it was," Rob said thoughtfully.

"I wish I could ask her. Mum might like to know about it."

Luke got his wish the next day, after the powwow broke up. Colonel Macleod strode down to their campfire, Potts at his side. "These are Blackfoot," the officer said. "Somehow they learned that we have a Native lad with us. The chief would like to speak with him."

Luke stood, swaying a little. "I'll talk to him. Where is he?"

"There's only one problem," the colonel replied. "He expects you to go over to their camp. Potts tells me that, because this man is a chief, it's what's customary."

Rob shook his head. "Uh-uh. No sir. Luke's not going over there."

"I wouldn't order you to go, Luke, even though Jerry here tells me you would be quite safe. He's even volunteered to go with you and stay as long as you're over there."

"Luke," Rob began to protest, but before he could make any kind of argument, Luke scowled and interrupted.

"Rob, I want to do this. It's time I made up my own mind about some things."

Without another word, Rob turned on his heel and walked away.

CHAPTER TWENTY

The camp was out of sight by the time Rob stopped walking and sat on a rock to stare at the horizon, his emotions swirling. *Something's happened to Luke. He's never once done anything I didn't want him to, and never once did he talk to me that way. What if they keep him. The colonel wouldn't want that, but there's more of them than there is of us, and he wants to be friends with the Indians.* Rob tried to be angry with Luke, but he couldn't. He was too afraid that Luke might not want to come back.

Rob walked slowly back to the fire. He had no idea how long he had been sitting there, but the sun had reached its zenith and was on its way back down. He began to walk faster: maybe Luke was back.

As Rob passed the line of picketed horses, he saw that Chris was still missing. Clearly, Luke hadn't returned.

Up ahead he could see Colonel Macleod talking with some of the men. There was no sign of the Blackfoot. He raced back to Sam, and without bothering with a saddle, leaped on her back and galloped up the hill. Rob brought her to a halt when they reached the top and saw that the Blackfoot camp was still there. There were ten circles of colourful teepees, each with its own campfire. The nearest one was also the largest. There was a small crowd of women and children standing on both sides of it, and around its campfire were two circles of blanket-wrapped men; Luke and Potts were seated with them. Aware that all eyes were staring at him, Rob started wishing he were back in camp.

An elderly man with long, grey braids gestured to him and spoke to a young one, who leaped to his feet and ran over to Rob to lead his horse closer. The elder spoke then, in a long series of remarks, and Potts translated. "Luke's brother is welcome. Come sit."

They made room for Rob beside Luke, who looked at him, his eyes filled with questions. Rob was hesitant to even whisper to Luke, for the elder was speaking again. It was a short speech that Potts translated. "He says we will meet again soon."

As the men rose and began to drift away, there were murmurs among the women. They were staring at Rob, and a few of them began to titter behind their hands. He looked at Potts uneasily. "They're admiring your red hair."

The elder rose and came forward to put his hand on Luke's shoulder. Rob couldn't understand the words, but knew that he was speaking them with a lot of feeling. When he finished Potts said, "He says you're welcome here anytime."

Rob was stunned when he heard Luke say, "Thank you, Grandfather," and Potts translated again.

The three of them rode back to camp in silence. Even when Potts parted from them and they tethered their horses, they still didn't speak. Rob was determined not to ask questions, but when Luke started for the wagon he could stand it no longer.

"Well, what was that all about?"

"I just wanted to know why the chief wanted to see me."

Rob was impatient. "I don't mean that. I mean why're you calling him grandfather?"

Luke shrugged. "He thinks he is. I just thought it might make him feel good."

Rob was stunned. Had Luke found his Native family? He tried to swallow, but his throat was too dry. Instead he croaked, "Why'd he think that? You don't even know if you're Blackfoot."

"Potts thinks I am."

"Potts! What's he know about it?"

Luke hesitated a moment before he said, "After you found Denny and me, and we were riding back, he was asking me about the horses we're looking for; and before I knew it, I told him all about it."

"So?"

"I was telling him about Mum and the pedal organ she wants shipped, and you and the saddle and Dad; and just like Denny, he asks what I want. And all of a sudden I knew. I want to know who I am."

Rob felt a stab of pain. "And I guess, just like magic, old Potts could tell you."

It was plain that Luke was tired, but he patiently replied, "Riding back with Potts yesterday, he tried a few words of different Indian talk, and I remembered some words I heard a long time past. He said they were Blackfoot."

Rob was more worried than ever. "Luke, that don't mean a thing far as this bunch goes. That don't prove you belong to this tribe."

"I know that," Luke said wearily. "But the chief said that about ten years ago some Cree sneaked up on his village early one morning, and before they could do anything about it, they shot some of the warriors and stole some of the women and children."

"And you and your mother might have been one of them?"

Luke nodded and began to climb into the wagon. "The chief's son was killed and his wife and little boy disappeared."

Rob's thoughts were churning. He didn't want to believe that Luke belonged to these people. Luke was his brother, not theirs. "Bet Potts put that idea in your head," he snapped.

"Potts is a good man, Rob. I told him one day I thought I might try to find my mother's people. He was just trying to help."

"Help! I'd like to give him some help."

Luke had stretched out on his pallet of blankets. He raised his head and looked at Rob, surprise in his tired eyes. "Why are you so fired up, Rob?"

He didn't know how to answer and couldn't bring himself to say, "Because you're my brother, and I don't want you going to live anywhere besides our place. I don't want to have to see Mum's face if I go back alone."

He tried to think of something to say, but Luke had fallen asleep.

Luke didn't cough during the night nearly as much as he had the past couple of weeks. For that, Rob was grateful enough to smile at his brother when he opened his eyes. "You find out what that stuff was you swallowed yesterday?"

Luke sat up, yawned widely, and scratched his head. "Soon as I got to the camp over there, that old one came up and made me take some more. Potts said it was something from the pine trees — something she scraped off under the bark and boiled."

Rob screwed up his face and stuck out his tongue. "Sounds delicious."

"Nope. But I'm sure obliged to her just the same."

Rob felt like he and Luke were in tune again, and didn't want to spoil it. He decided not to ask Luke the dreaded question, whether or not he intended to stay with the Blackfoot. Instead, he said, "Time to rustle our bones then. I think we're leaving soon's we're packed up." He paused before he climbed from the wagon to give Luke a chance to say he wasn't going. When he didn't Rob jumped out, feeling a bit lighter.

Pierre and Bruce had a fire going and the pot on for tea. The smell of frying meat and dough floated from the fire, reminding Rob that he was starving. The two men looked up as he approached.

"Luke okay?" the red haired trooper asked. "I thought he looked a might peaked last night."

"I think he was just tired," Rob replied. "He seems real good this morning."

"Well, I'm thinking that's all to the good," another trooper said, reaching for a stick to stir the fire. "We're going to need every man we have if we meet up with those whiskey traders today."

"Today?" Rob asked eagerly. "We really are moving out then?"

"I heard the colonel tell Brisebois that he expects we should reach Fort Whoop-Up by nightfall."

Bruce snorted derisively. "Tell him the rest, man."

"Don't mean too much. That Potts feller seems to think the fort's gonna be empty. He claims they would've heard we're coming and lit outta there fast as their horses could gallop."

Rob didn't want to believe that. They had to be there, and the horses, too. "We would've cut their trail. Nobody we came across lately has seen any horses with two or three men. Not even the Indians."

The trooper waved the stick he had been using into the air. "When you been around long as I have, you'll learn folks don't always tell the truth. And that's a fact."

"You could be right — for once," Bruce agreed. "You take that Morrow or whatever his name was. You know, the one who told Colonel French he'd been to Fort Whoop-Up, and then it turns out he didn't know which way from nowhere. He tells that he saw a herd driven by some men, but can you believe him?"

Rob was spared from his urge to reply when Luke climbed from the wagon and came toward him. He was greeted by a chorus of "How're you feeling?" but their words were cut short when the pretty Native girl approached, her eyes on the ground modestly. She touched Luke's shoulder, and when he spun around she offered him the gourd she was carrying.

Luke took it, squinting his eyes and wrinkling his nose, and the girl laughed delightedly. He tried to hand the gourd back to her, but she shook her head, and used her hand to make drinking motions. Sighing deeply, Luke tilted his head back and drank until the gourd was empty, then pounded his feet in a frenzied dance. This time Rob and the other men joined her in a hearty laugh.

Luke returned the gourd to the girl, and though she accepted it, she didn't leave. They stood in silence, and suddenly she reached out to pass one hand down the side of Luke's face. Then turned and ran away.

If Luke was embarrassed by this display of affection, he didn't show it. He sauntered to the fire, wiping his mouth. With a chuckle, Bruce said, "I guess whatever that was it must have tasted pretty bad."

Luke raised his eyebrows. "What makes you say that?"

After the camp was cleaned up, and the two boys saddled their horses, Rob said teasingly, "Looks like you got to be pretty well acquainted with the little gal that carried that drink to you."

Luke still didn't seem embarrassed. He shrugged his shoulders and said, "Yep."

For an instant, Rob had the weird feeling that he'd shrunk and Luke had grown taller. Irritated, he snapped at his brother. "You sure act funny, Luke. Wonder what that old woman put in that drink besides tree bark."

Luke swung into his saddle. "Don't know."

Rob knew they were making good time for two reasons. Mr. Conrad was far behind with Denny's group, so there were no oxen plodding with them, and the trail was wide and clear.

It was early afternoon when Rob spotted a mass of treetops in the distance, a sure sign that they must be nearing water. Potts and two constables had ridden ahead, and they returned an hour later to report that they had almost reached the meeting point of the two rivers. Rob choked up with excitement: this was the spot where the whiskey traders had built Fort Whoop-Up! Colonel Macleod called a halt and ordered that the cannon be brought up.

Potts called out, "Fort is empty. Waste of powder."

"I do trust your judgement, Jerry," Macleod said. "But I think it best if I see for myself."

While the gun was being brought up, Luke and Rob rode up to join the two men. The hill where they stood was too low to see over the stockade; but the outside appeared to be built from long, peeled logs. Rising above them were bastions at each of the four corners.

When the gun was in place, the colonel, Potts, and four troopers rode down and presented themselves at the double front gate of the fort.

The troopers rode back less than half an hour later. One of them, Constable Patterson, slid off his horse and announced that there was only a caretaker down there, and he had invited the colonel and Potts to supper. Patterson's grin was huge when he announced that he and the other three men were to bunk in the fort to make sure no whiskey traders came back.

"I'll be thinking of you poor lads tonight when it's sleeping I am, in a bunk, warm and off the ground."

Rob and Luke didn't stay to hear the rude responses: they slapped their mounts on the rumps and galloped recklessly down the slope. The front gate stood open, and Potts was just inside waiting for the colonel who stood talking to a stooped, elderly Métis. The colonel stopped talking, and raised his eyebrows as the boys rode in slowly. "Why am I not surprised to see you?"

Before he could even open his mouth, Potts answered the question Rob was about to ask. A jerk of his head indicated the caretaker. "Doesn't know anything about a herd of horses, he says."

Rob nodded and, with Luke following, turned his horse to plod back up the hill. "The end of the trail, I guess," Luke said.

Rob couldn't bring himself to reply.

CHAPTER TWENTY-ONE

Rob and Luke helped set up the camp for the night in silence. Word was that they would be moving to a more permanent location in the morning. It wasn't until nightfall, when they had retired to their tent, that they faced their situation.

Rob sat on his blankets pulling off his boots. "It's October, Luke, and getting mighty cold. I know you're feeling a lot better now, but I think we have to spend the winter here." He felt a flash of anger when it occurred to him that Luke might be glad — he would be close to his Blackfoot people.

Rob was ashamed of himself when Luke frowned worriedly. "What if our letter got lost?"

"That wouldn't happen. Besides, when Mum and Dad get wind of the troopers getting back to Fort Ellice they'll be down there to hear the latest news. After they find out we stayed on with the troops, they'll figure on us coming home in the spring."

Luke fell asleep quickly; but Rob lay awake wondering if Dad and Mum were thinking and wondering and worrying, too.

In the morning, Colonel Macleod addressed his troops. "Every one of you know that we have a daunting task ahead. With fewer than two hundred of us, we are going to clear this land of whiskey traders and outlaws and bring peace among four warring tribes of Indians. This means each of us must be vigilant and dedicated to his task. Our first order of the day will be to build a fort. Jerry Potts has advised me to move our camp to the valley of the Oldman River, which isn't far away. We will first ford two smaller rivers." He paused, waiting for questions. When none were forthcoming, the colonel ordered, "Mount up."

The line was quick to move again, since they were eager to get started. A fort would mean cabins and regular meals. They followed the scout to an area more lush than any they had seen. There was plenty of dead grass for the animals to graze at their leisure and a sparkling, clean river winding through a forest of pine and spruce and aspen. Buffalo could be seen roaming a short distance away on the open prairie, which gave way to magnificent mountains in the distance. Every trooper, officer, and cart driver set to work with enthusiasm. Even before the last tent was erected, axes were ringing against the tall cottonwoods needed to begin building the fort.

Rob and Luke watered and hobbled all of the horses, and then dug pits for the fires that would later cook their dinners. Finished with those tasks, they stripped branches from the trees that were felled. They went to bed that night too tired to talk or worry about the coming winter.

A few days later, when Denny and the weary horses, oxen, and wagons arrived, he expressed his delight in the camp in a decidedly unmilitary way by jumping from his horse and turning cartwheels. "By thunder," he cried, "this must be Heaven!"

Denny's words may have urged the carpenters to even further efforts: in less than two weeks, three long, rough log barracks with mud for plaster had been built and set in a horseshoe formation facing the river. At the end of it, a log enclosure was made to corral the horses. All of these were being built, while other men were straining to dig deep trenches to put up tall cottonwoods and create a wall around the wooden buildings. Such niceties as a cookhouse, a carpenter shop, a blacksmith shop, and bunks for the cabins were to come later. For now, it was luxury enough to fold up their tents and sleep inside.

Before they were finished, big groups of Blackfoot came to trade but were referred to the store Conrad had built nearby; the men of the North-West Mounted Police had nothing to trade. After five months of travel, though, they were finally paid, and could purchase buckskin shirts and breeches to replace their ruined uniforms.

Stories about Potts circulated around the campfire every night — some almost hard to believe, though they were sworn true by the drivers who had brought up the huge wagons from Conrad's store and stayed on to build a trading post.

One, called Duval, claimed he had been working at a Fort McKenzie south of the boundary line, a bit over thirty years ago, when Potts lived there as a child. "You most likely know he was but a little one when his father was shot and his mother left him at the fort where they had lived." When he saw that everyone knew that story Duval, went on. "While Potts was still small, she went back to the fort to live with a very bad man — name of Alexander Harvey. Everyone feared him, and he did very bad things. Good for him, he died when our friend Potts was still small — about seven, I think. That's when I first knew him. He had learned much, and even so young he was known as a hunter and tracker. This he learns from his Blackfoot people."

It was Denny who filled in some of the blanks in the history of Jerry Potts one night. "Conrad speaks highly of him. He didn't mention anything about this bad fellow, but he did say that Potts also had spent a good bit of time with the Blood tribe — part of the Blackfoot Nation, I believe. That was a few years before Dawson took him in."

"How did he become a scout then?" Rob asked.

"Dawson travelled around a great deal, trading among the tribes. He was a good man, well respected and, as a result, our Mr. Potts came to know several of the Indian languages, as well as his own Blackfoot; so he often was called upon to be an interpreter as well as a scout."

"What happened to Mr. Dawson?" a trooper asked.

Surprisingly, Luke answered the question. "I know. Potts told me that Mr. Dawson was a great father and an important fur trader at Fort Benton, but he fell through the floor in his house one night and his legs were bad ever after. He finally had to quit working and go back to Scotland."

When one of the men asked what the scout did after that, Luke continued. "He was already a scout and an interpreter. He spent a lot of time with the Blackfoot people, too. They named him Bear Child."

One of the drivers, a Métis who, until now, hadn't spoken, said, "It's a name the Blackfoot give only to those who have earned it, for he has fought at their side many times and with honour."

Rob said nothing, but he was getting just a bit tired of hearing stories about the great Jerry Potts. *Bad enough he's been filling Luke's head with the wonders of being a Blackfoot without everybody else making us think he's the best at everything he does. There has to be a way to keep Luke from spending so much time with him.*

A few days later, Rob realized that keeping Luke away from the scout was going to be easier than he thought: he'd learned that Inspector Walsh and Potts were going to take a half dozen men and drive the weakest of the horses and cattle south of the border where there would be feed, and warmer temperatures than along the Oldman River. However, the very day that they were ready to start off, a dignified elderly Blackfoot rode into camp. Everyone stopped work and watched as Colonel Macleod greeted the man and Potts listened to his words.

When the elderly man finished, Jerry turned to the colonel and said, "He is Three Bulls, a chief. Four men have a cabin about fifteen miles north of here along a dry creek bed. They came to his village and made him sell them two of his best horses. They gave him two jugs of whiskey but he threw them away."

The colonel turned to Inspector Crozier, who was standing nearby. "Take Potts and ten of your men to find these whiskey traders."

Inspector Crozier was the leader of F Troop, and Sub-Inspector Denny nearly fell over his feet in his haste to reach his superior's side. "I'd very much like to go, sir."

Crozier raised his eyebrows and hesitated. "Get ready then, and chose the rest."

"Whiskey traders," Luke whispered to Rob. "I thought they all were supposed to be gone until spring."

Rob was thinking. *Colonel Macleod's been good to us and mighty forgiving for the times we stayed when we shouldn't have, but I expect he has a limit.*

"You're thinking we should follow them, ain't you?" Luke asked eagerly.

"If it's only fifteen miles, we won't need to take a tent, so we can go ahead of them. Nobody will notice if we just ride off: they'll think we're going hunting."

Luke had run toward the corral. "We better get going."

The sun radiated from the deep blue sky as both Chris and Sam cantered along easily, pleased to be free of the corral's confines. Rob's heart was beating faster with each mile that fell behind them. He wouldn't allow himself to consider the possibility that they wouldn't find the cabin. There was only one dry creek bed to the north and, as Luke had pointed out, sun or not, there was bound to be smoke drifting from a chimney.

Luke was right. After riding for little more than an hour, they saw a thin trail of grey rising above a thick stand of spruce and pine about a mile ahead. As they slowly moved closer, they saw no sign of life. If there were a cabin, it was hidden in the trees. They pulled their horses to a stop and considered their next steps.

"We got guns," Luke said slowly.

"Don't be daft, Luke," Rob said, almost laughing. "We don't have any right to arrest them or anything. We're looking for our horses. What we got to do is find a way to get into the trees and see if these varmints are the ones that have them."

Luke nodded and looked around. "Over there." He said, pointing to a narrow ditch nearby that seemed to lead right into the trees a hundred yards away.

Rob and Luke slid from their horses, leaving the reins hanging. Ducking low, they headed for the ditch. The snow, leftover from a light fall a week earlier, was mushy and was barely deep enough for cover if they had to lie down and hide. They both sucked in their breath with the suddenness of the cold inside the shade of the thick woods. After taking the time to properly survey the area, they followed the gently sloping ditch for more than a hundred feet through the trees, halting suddenly when the sound of a banging door broke the silence.

Rob turned to Luke and whispered, "We must be close to the cabin."

The woods had thinned and, slipping from tree to tree, the two boys peered through them. Rob stopped so suddenly that Luke banged into him. There was a break in the trees ahead, and just beyond it was a corral with a herd of horses inside. And one of them was Smokey!

"Rob!" Luke whispered, his eyes wide and shining.

Rob couldn't answer: his mouth had gone dry. They stood together, motionless for a long moment before he could whisper, "Let's get closer."

They still hadn't spotted the cabin, but they tried to make themselves as small as possible as they crept toward the corral. A dozen feet away Rob stopped and counted. There were about twenty horses — a mixture of browns and blacks — besides those with the tell-tale grey coats. All the mares were there. Standing with his head high now, Smokey was sniffing the air and stomping his hoofs restlessly.

Before Rob could stop him, Luke said, "Oh, Smokey boy!" The stallion began to run back and forth in the enclosure. He galloped to the back of the corral and raced forward as though planning to jump the fence, but the corral was too crowded for him to gain enough distance to leap.

The mares were excited and began running around. A door banged again. Rob and Luke ducked behind a tree and listened. "Fool horses!" a gravely voice grumbled. "Don't know why he don't want to get rid of 'em."

A tall man with thick, rounded shoulders and a full black beard slouched to the corral, a shotgun swinging in his hand. He paused when he reached the horses, looked inside the enclosure, and walked around it. The horses were still milling around nervously, but slowly. After another look inside and around, the man turned and stomped into the trees.

"What're we going to do?" Luke asked.

Rob slowly let out the breath he'd been holding. "We got to sit right here until Crozier and Potts and Denny and the rest get here. We just got to hope they didn't change their minds about leaving right away."

"Let's get closer to the corral," Luke said.

"All right, but we can't let Smokey see us or he'll try to jump the fence and might break a leg."

Cautiously, they slipped forward and crouched again, less than ten feet from the horses. Rob stared at them lovingly. There was Billie with her long nose and one white foreleg; and the filly his mother had named

Stormy because she was foaled during a thunder storm; and…. He caught a movement from the corner of his eye. Rob turned his head swiftly.

CHAPTER
TWENTY-TWO

Leaning against a half-dead spruce stood the wolfer with the long scar on his face. He was pointing his rifle right at them.

"Lookin' for something?" the wolfer sneered, revealing blackened teeth. His eyes were cold.

Rob was shaking with fear, but wouldn't allow himself to show it. His mind worked quickly. *There has to be a way to get out of this. If these are the men that killed all the people in that Indian village, they're pure evil. But right now if they do anything to us, they'd be easy to track down with the snow on the ground. Maybe we could talk our way out of this.*

"Well?" the wolfer snarled.

"I guess you know what we're looking for: our stallion. We need him."

The wolfer's eyebrows shot up in surprise. "Well, I'll be! You're the two whelps from that dirt farm back east!"

"Dirt farm!" Luke yelped. "We got...." He fell silent when Rob jabbed him with an elbow.

The wolfer straightened and looked around. "Where's your folks?"

Rob had a plan. Trying to look innocent, he said, "They're a few miles east looking for our horses. They're going to be mighty grateful that you found them. I expect you'll be welcome at our ranch any time you come by."

For a moment he thought his plan might work. *If this dunderhead is as confused as he looks, it might be a while before they figure out what to do with us, and by then Potts and the rest might be here.*

Rob couldn't tell right away if his plan worked or not. The wolfer stood staring at them, then jerked his head to the left. "Get along," he ordered.

Prodding them forward, the man directed them between the trees until they reached a small clearing where a cabin stood. It had a sagging roof and an air of abandonment. The thin trail of smoke they'd seen from afar rose from its chimney.

When they reached the door the wolfer cried out, "Look what I found!"

The door was jerked open, and the round-shouldered man leaped out, pistol in his hand.

"Where'd you find 'em?" he asked with a scowl on his unshaven face.

"Told you to take a good look, didn't I? Well this is what you missed — the young'uns from that farm by Fort Ellice, and I wasn't even looking for 'em. I was checking out our stash."

"Well, quit crowing, Kamoose. Where'd you find 'em?"

Rob felt his whole body grow cold. Kamoose! Kamoose Taylor — the worst outlaw in the West! He inched closer to Luke, who was staring at the wolfer.

"Get inside," Kamoose said, pushing each boy with the rifle.

They entered the dusty cabin and coughed. The air reeked of stale tobacco smoke and burned food. There were two wooden stools and a table with three legs tilted against the peeling wall. A small fireplace was burning brightly. "Get down," Kamoose ordered, pushing both boys to the floor. Rob looked at Luke to see if he was as scared as he was, but he couldn't tell. Luke was staring straight ahead, ignoring the men.

Putting his rifle down, Kamoose said, "They tell me their folks are out looking for the horses, too. Don't know as if I believe 'em, but for sure somebody's gonna be looking for these young'uns."

"I tol' ya that herd out there was gonna be too much

trouble. We ain't even been able to sell 'em. We shoulda turned 'em loose a long time ago."

"If the police are buying, they're worth about two hundred a head and the stallion, maybe four. That's why we didn't turn 'em loose."

"Then why didn't we take 'em up to that fort they're building and sell 'em?"

Instead of answering, Kamoose jumped to his feet so quickly that the stool he had been seated on fell over. "The horses are stirred up again. I'm taking a look this time."

The second wolfer nodded. "Maybe somebody looking for these." A jerk of his head indicated Rob and Luke.

"Or somebody aiming to find the whiskey," Kamoose said over his shoulder as he left the cabin.

Rob relaxed. All he and Luke had to do was wait. It was probably Crozier and his men disturbing the mares. He thought about who would be first to find Luke and him — Denny maybe or Potts. Didn't matter who it was, he'd be very happy to see him.

The wolfer was pacing around the little room. When the door burst open suddenly he whirled around, and reached for the pistol in his belt.

He was too late. In the door stood Crozier, Denny behind him, their weapons drawn. They moved inside. "You're under arrest," the officer said calmly. "Hand over your gun."

A constable followed the two officers inside and roped the wolfers' hands behind their backs. In an instant Denny was beside the two boys. "Are you all right?" he asked anxiously. He helped them to their feet. "Are you quite all right?"

Resisting the urge to hug him, Rob laughed. "We're fine, aren't we Luke?"

Luke nodded. His eyes were shining happily.

Crozier scowled. "Don't coddle them, Denny," he snapped. "When we return to the fort they will have a great deal of explaining to do. But I will ask Colonel Macleod to be mindful of the good you two have done now and then, including healing my horse." He walked through the open doorway and said, over his shoulder, "And now we're even."

Rob was too relieved to be worried about getting reprimanded by the commander. After this, nothing worse could happen. He called after Crozier. "We heard something, sir," he said. "I think they have whiskey hidden somewhere close by. Kamoose Taylor just went out to check on it."

"Kamoose Taylor and whiskey, as well. This will be a red letter day for us," commented the officer, who looked very pleased.

Denny said, "The men are already searching the woods, looking for their cache."

"Our horses are here, too." Rob couldn't stop grinning. "I think every one of them's here."

"Bully for you two," Denny said. He looked like he was going to say more when they heard loud shouts followed by a half dozen gunshots. A moment later wildly running horses streamed past the open door. Rob and Luke were outside before Denny reached the door and were stunned to see their herd and the other horses from the corral racing around in all directions. In the flying dust, Kamoose flew past, bent low over Smokey. Two constables were giving chase, but Smokey was far ahead racing up a low hill. Another horse appeared from his right. On its back Potts was taking aim with a pistol. Rob heard Luke's hushed "Oh, no," when the gunshots reached their ears. Kamoose jerked Smokey's head sideways then, turning him back down the hill. With Potts on one side and two constables closing in on the other, he had no choice but to go in a third direction bringing Smokey closer to the cabin.

Crozier and Denny were beside the cabin, their rifles at their shoulders now. "No wait! Please don't shoot," Rob pleaded.

"Watch," Luke said. He put his fingers in his mouth and gave a sharp two-note whistle. Smokey promptly slid to a halt sending Kamoose flying over his head. The mares also slowed, then stopped running in circles. Both

Rob and Luke laughed aloud as they raced toward the horses, none of them wearing bridles.

"Like old times," Rob said and leaped on the back of a light, grey mare. He wound his hands in her mane and turned her head toward Smokey. Luke followed on her twin.

"You drive a hard bargain," Colonel Macleod said. "But two hundred each is a good price." He smiled and held out a paper. "This is a note payable to your father, to be collected at Fort Ellice. He can use it to buy goods, or, if he'd rather, money can be sent to him from Winnipeg."

Rob was elated by the thought of going home, but weaving through his delight was the sad thought of leaving these men. Saying goodbye wouldn't be easy. He found it a bit surprising that Potts was the one who made him feel better when he swept one deer hide covered arm around, indicating both men and fort, and said. "Maybe someday you will be one, like these. Then you come back."

Rob couldn't help liking the scout a little even if he had changed Luke's feelings toward him and their parents. But if it weren't for Potts, Kamoose could have gotten away. And Potts had kept his shots high, careful not to hit Smokey. It was also Potts who was going to help them get home, at least part.

Rob was ready to start off the moment Colonel Macleod agreed to buy the herd — except for Smokey. Luke agreed that their parents should know about the money right away so they could buy supplies for winter, and plan for spring. William McKay would let them buy goods on credit, but they knew their father wouldn't, unless he was sure he could pay for them later. They had to get home. They just had to.

One morning, Potts brought his tea to their campfire and sat on a rock beside them. "Walsh and me are taking horses to Sun River in a couple of days. Me, I'm taking a pack horse for myself. After Sun River, I got to go east for a time."

Both boys stared at him wide-eyed. "How far east?" Rob asked.

Potts shrugged. "Far enough. Want to come?"

Luke and Rob wasted no time in running to the office Colonel Macleod had set up in one of the long, low cabins. The commander was doubtful at first, and both Denny and Crozier were almost angry. It's late October, they argued paying no attention to the boys. And the cold had dropped to forty below at this time last year. There could be bad storms, as well as hostile tribes between here and Fort Ellice. "Right," Denny said. "And just where is Potts going?"

Colonel Macleod had an answer for that. "Potts

misses his wives and his children. He has a small ranch somewhere east of Benton. After he and Walsh get the stock to Sun River, he plans to travel to it and bring his family back here."

Crozier looked incredulous. "He intends to bring his family back here in the winter?"

"Yes, and I was pleased to hear him say as much," the colonel snapped. "It means he intends to stay with us. He's a valuable asset for the job we have to do. And Conrad has said he will send a letter along for Rob and Luke to give to a man in his store at Benton. It will instruct him to keep an eye out for trappers or traders — anyone going up as far as Fort Ellice. They'll be paid to take the boys there."

Denny and Crozier were silent.

"See here," Colonel Macleod said quietly, "I haven't made the decision lightly, to allow two youngsters to go back across a trail that proved to be so difficult for even well protected, fit men. But Jerry Potts is another story. He can smell water where we cannot find it. He can find game where there is none. He can find his way in the dark in places he has never been before. He has said he will look after the boys. I am satisfied that they will be safe. And knowing these lads, I fear if we made them stay here, they would find a way to go home on their own."

* * *

The journey down to Sun River seemed to take forever to Rob, though it was only a bit over a week. The path had not been easy — there were heavy snow storms on two of the days — but they were using good prairie horses, some bought from the Blackfoot and some that had been part of the McCann herd. Rob was proud of the way they behaved and of Smokey. It felt good to ride him again. He and Luke were taking turns putting their saddle on him each morning. They were more farewells after they reached Sun River, when he and Luke left for the East with Potts. He liked Walsh and the rest of the constables in his troop, and felt a warm glow inside when realized they liked Luke and him as well.

Rob had heard Potts tell Inspector Walsh they would go straight east, and they were going east all right, but a bit to the north as well. After two days of uneventful riding and camping, Rob began to wonder: what was Potts up to? Dark thoughts began to float in his mind. *Could Potts be so set on having Luke join up with the Blackfoot that he would take us somewhere to get rid of me?* Rob felt his face go red at the thought, and he told himself not to be daft.

They were grateful for the sun that shone, despite the time of year. "This is great, isn't it, Rob," Luke said when they camped on the fourth night after leaving Walsh and his men. "Not like poking along with all those oxen and sick horses."

Rob agreed, even though he had no sense of how far they had come. He decided to ask. "Mr. Potts ..." he began and paused when the scouts drooping black moustache twitched.

"Name's Potts or Jerry or Bear Child," he said. "No mister."

Rob cleared his throat. "I just wanted to ask how much longer to Fort Benton. Do you have an idea?"

"Not going to Fort Benton," he said.

Rob was alarmed. "Then where are we going?"

"What you think?"

Rob looked at the scout, then at Luke and back to Potts. All his fears came to the fore at that moment, and without thinking about consequences, he spit out, "I think you're up to something sneaky. You want to take us someplace besides Benton. But I won't let you take Luke away: he's my brother."

Luke was astonished, and a surprised expression appeared on Potts's face. "Take Luke?"

Luke grabbed Rob's arm. "What're you talking about?"

Rob sat on a rock and hung his head. "I don't know. I just — well you're always talking to Potts and about your Blackfoot family. I've been afraid...."

Potts shook his head, and poked the fire while Luke explained. "Potts and I have been talking, Rob. He told me how it was when he didn't know if he was Blackfoot or Scottish. It wasn't easy for him, but it helped me think. I'm not ever going to leave you and Mum and Dad. Oh, I might leave for some time when I'm grown; but I'll always come back when I can. Potts showed me how the Blackfoot and Sioux and the rest are getting pushed around, and I want to help when I'm done with growing. I think maybe I'll become a policeman and come back to help them, like Colonel Macleod. That might take a few years, though, Rob."

Rob didn't know what to say. There wasn't anything to say, except that he was sorry he had held back such bad feelings. But he couldn't say that, and Potts spared him the necessity of saying anything when he held out a tin plate of deer meat and potatoes.

"Eat," he said.

Both boys knew they had steadily travelled northeast for more than two weeks, but they didn't want to bother Potts by asking how far they'd come. Happily, the weather had been good, though cold, and they had more than enough blankets. They had shared their blankets with their horses. Potts still said nothing when they saw a boundary marker, nor later when Roche Percée appeared in the eastern distance. They talked it over then when they camped, after Potts had fallen asleep. "We should be able to make it on our own now," Luke said.

Rob agreed. "I'd sure like to have Mum and Dad meet Potts, though, and be able to thank him. I know they'd want to for all he's done for us."

"He's got a ways to go," Luke argued. "Let's tell him thanks and go on by ourselves."

Right at that moment, Potts poked his head into their tent. "Sleep," he ordered. "Morning comes and we ride hard to Fort Ellice."

It was Rob's day to ride Smokey, and when he saw the fort in the distance, it was hard not to let the stallion run. Today they had come more than seventy miles, though, and even so special a stallion like Smokey would be tired. Beside Rob, Luke's face wore a look of eagerness as he rode. Potts was behind, leading the pack horse and Sam. As they drew closer to the fort, he called out, "Go on ahead. I'll be along."

With that order, both boys kicked their mounts and flew ahead. When they galloped inside the gates, William McKay dashed out of his office. "Luke, Rob!" he cried out, eyes wide with disbelief. When they reached his side, he grabbed each boy around the middle and hauled them out of their saddles. Hugging them both closely, he spoke in a choked whisper. "I almost gave you up for lost." Releasing them, he said more loudly,

"But not your folks. No, sir, not your folks. They knew you'd be back."

"How are they?" Rob asked. "They all right? Did they get the letters we sent with Inspector Jarvis?"

McKay nodded. "They spent a lot of time with the inspector, and except for missing their boys, they've been all right; and now, I guess they'll be more than all right." The chief factor yanked a huge, blue-dotted square of cloth out of his pocket and wiped his eyes.

Potts had ridden into the fort leading Sam and the pack horse. "He with you?" asked McKay.

"He is," Rob said with an affectionate grin. "This is Mis— This is Jerry Potts. He brought us home."

"He's going to his ranch just east of Fort Benton," Luke added. "But first he came north to bring us home."

Still on his horse and holding both sets of reins, Potts wore his usual unreadable expression as he looked down at the group of people that had gathered around.

"Did he now?" McKay said. Without taking his eyes from Potts, he said, "From what I've heard about you, Mr. Potts, I'd say you had a very safe journey."

Potts stared down at McKay, heaved a sigh and said, "Not mister. Names Jerry or Potts."

"Or Bear Child," Luke added.

"I'll remember that," McKay replied. "If you ever

need somewhere to stay, Bear Child, there'll always be a bunk for you here."

Potts nodded and turned his horse to follow Rob and Luke as they waved and rode back through the gate.

Rob held the reins tightly, not wanting Smokey to have his head lest he leave Luke and Potts in his dust. Even so, he arrived first in front of the cabin doorway. The clatter of hoof beats scattered the squawking chickens in all directions, and the door flew open. In seconds both Rob and Luke were at their mother's side; she was smiling and laughing, with tears streaming down her cheeks.

Hugging each boy, long moments passed in silence before Susan McCann stepped back and wiped her eyes on her white apron. "Dad's fine," she said. "He's in the back field loading wood on the stoneboat for the fire. He'll be that happy to see you both." She stopped to wipe her eyes again, and looking up to see Potts sitting quietly on his mount.

Although he was impatient to see his father, Rob quickly introduced Potts and told his mother that the scout had brought them home.

Susan reached up for Pott's hand and said, "Thank you. We'll never be able to repay you."

Plainly embarrassed, Potts said nothing, and Rob's mother added, "You look like a man that might know his way around a kitchen, Mr. Potts. Maybe you wouldn't mind coming in and helping me turn that big hunk of meat I have over the fire."

Potts swung from his horse. "Well now," he said, "I might just do that, Mrs. McCann, but the name's Jerry or Potts — not mister."

"Thank you, Jerry," Rob's mother said. "But the name's Susan, not Mrs. McCann."

Laughing aloud, both Rob and Luke allowed their mounts to run as they crossed the familiar fields. In the distance, they could see John McCann bending and straightening as he picked up snow covered chunks of wood and tossed them into a pile. When they drew closer he stood and shaded his eyes from the sun. Suddenly, he began to run, stumbling and almost falling on the uneven ground, but his boys had leaped from their horses and were there to catch him before he did. This time the hugs were bone crushing. When they were finally released Luke said, "We found Smokey, Dad!"

"I see you did," John choked out.

Rob reached inside his shirt and carefully brought out the certificate for the sale of the herd and handed it to his father.

John McCann looked at the paper, then back at Rob and Luke as though he could not believe what he read. Then he shook his head, pocketed the paper, and said, "Well done, lads." Putting an arm around the shoulders of each boy, he said, "Let's go up to the house and see what Mum's having for supper. We can finish hauling wood tomorrow."

It was good to be home.

AUTHOR'S NOTE

Led in the beginning by Colonel George A. French, the three hundred men who were sent to bring law and order to 300,000 square miles of unsettled, lawless prairie, were ill-equipped for the endless series of obstacles they encountered. The streams of fresh water they expected to find didn't materialize; they often went hungry; they fought mosquitoes, locusts, rain, and freezing cold; and their handsome uniforms turned to rags before they reached their goal. Their complaints were bitter, but quiet, and no one threatened to quit. They trusted and respected the men who led them — men whose names have not been forgotten, such as Colonel James Macleod and the dedicated men who served under him: Inspectors William D. Jarvis, James Walsh, C. E. Denny, and Lief Crozier, along with Sam Steele and his brothers, and Jerry Potts, their amazing scout.

Canada was a young country in 1874. Its inexperienced leaders in the East were kept busy organizing opposing political factions to create a stable government, and there was no law force beyond Winnipeg. The fur trading companies sometimes arrested an evildoer, but only if the crime affected their post, or their trade. They welcomed the arrival of the newly formed police force in the areas around the trading posts, even though the officers' prime mandate was to stop the practice of selling whiskey to the Natives, which they had been doing for two hundred years.

The young men, who had signed on for adventure with the newly formed North-West Mounted Police had no reason to be disappointed. They chased their first buffalo, were threatened by Native warriors, and saw the wonders nature had prepared for them: Roche Percée, with its wind eroded rocks; the eerie sacred valley that is now known as Writing-on-Stone Provincial Park; the endless stretches of treeless prairie; and most astonishing of all — the Rocky Mountains.

If any of the men joined in the hopes of finding work, they were rewarded beyond expectations. They chopped huge trees — to plant into the ground, making a stockade to surround their fort, and more for the buildings inside — and hunted for their food. All of that for very little pay that arrived infrequently, except for the promise of a grant of prairie land after their term of enlistment had ended.

Except for the two lads and their parents, the characters in *Shadow Riders* were once real, and events in the story were derived from books, diaries, journals, and pamphlets found in museums and libraries. In no way can be overstated the contribution of these courageous men to the building of Canada.

CHRONOLOGY

Early July 1874	Rob and Luke look for their stolen horses.
July 8	Three hundred policemen, plus Metis scouts and drivers, leave Fort Dufferin for the western prairies as the North-West Mounted Police.
July 14	The troops cross the Pembina River and head over the Missouri plateau; water, firewood, and food are scarce, and the horses are tiring.

July 19   Rob and Luke find North-West Mounted Police camp and join them on their march.

July 24-28   The troops arrive at Roche Percée for rest, good water, and food supplies. The force is split, with Inspector Jarvis and the Steele brothers leading a smaller contingent to Fort Ellice and onwards to Fort Edmonton, the two boys accompany the main force.

August 13-17   The troops arrive at Old Wives Lake, where there is poor water but some game, then they move to Old Wife's Creek where there is better water. The troops establish contact with the Sioux, set up Cripple Camp for sick and injured men.

August 24   The North-West Mounted Police cross the prairies into the Cypress Hills, where they sight and kill buffalo for food, meet hostile Natives on a trek to find the Belly River and Fort Whoop-Up, without success.

September 22

The troops move south to the Sweet Grass Hills, with winter weather setting in. Colonel French and Colonel Macleod travel to Fort Benton, Montana, for supplies.

September 24-26

In Fort Benton, they make contact with Ottawa and Colonel French is ordered back to Fort Ellice and Ottawa. They secure supplies and arrange further business with I.G. Baker & Co., and engage Jerry Potts as a scout who knew the terrain and Fort Whoop-Up's location.

October 9

Colonel Macleod travels with troops to Fort Whoop-Up and is invited in to dine by the caretaker, but no whiskey is found.

October 13	The troops vacate Fort Whoop-Up to set up a permanent North-West Mounted Police post to the north west on the Old Man River.
November	The two boys and Inspector Denny recover the stolen horses, and leave Fort Macleod with Jerry Potts for the return home.

SELECTED READING

Dempsey, Hugh A. *Firewater: The Impact of the Whisky Trade on the Blackfoot Nation*. Calgary: Fifth House, 2002.

Dempsey, Hugh A., ed. *William Parker: Mounted Policeman*. Calgary: Glenbow-Alberta Institute and Edmonton: Hurtig Publishers, 1973.

Denny, Sir Cecil E. *Denny's Trek: A Mountie's Memoir of the March West*. Surrey, BC: Heritage House Publishing, 2004.

Denny, Sir Cecil E. *The Law Marches West*. Toronto: J. M. Dent and Sons, 1972.

Murphy, James E. *Half Interest in the Silver Dollar: The Saga of Charles E. Conrad*. Missoula: Mountain Press Publishing Co., 1983.

Ross, David and Robin May. *The Royal Canadian Mounted Police 1873–1987*. London: Osprey Publishing, 1988.

Royal Canadian Mounted Police. *Opening Up the West: Being the Official Reports to Parliament of the Activities of the Royal North-West Mounted Police force from 1874–1881*. Toronto: Coles Canadiana Collection, 1973.

Touchie, Rodger D. *Bear Child: The Life and Times of Jerry Potts*. Victoria, BC: Heritage House, 2005.

ALSO BY
B.J. BAYLE

Battle Cry at Batoche
978-1-55002-717-4
$11.99

Ben and Charity Muldoon are fifteen-year-old twins who find themselves in the midst of politically charged events in the Saskatchewan River Valley in 1885. After befriending a Cree boy named Red Eagle, Ben eventually discovers that a confrontation between the North-West Mounted Police and the Natives, led by Louis Riel and Gabriel Dumont, is imminent. Caught between his loyalty to Red Eagle and the authority of a Hudson's Bay Company uncle he has never trusted, Ben must decide where his allegiance lies. But as he soon learns, when it comes to friendship, there is no taking sides.